Overnight Love

BECAUSE NAUGHTY CAN BE OH SO NICE.®

NE
LTD

By Nicole Edwards

The Alluring Indulgence Series
Kaleb
Zane
Travis
Holidays with the Walker Brothers
Ethan
Braydon
Sawyer
Brendon

The Austin Arrows Series
Rush
Kaufman

The Bad Boys of Sports Series
Bad Reputation
Bad Business

The Caine Cousins Series
Hard to Hold
Hard to Handle

The Club Destiny Series
Conviction
Temptation
Addicted
Seduction
Infatuation
Captivated
Devotion
Perception
Entrusted
Adored
Distraction

The Coyote Ridge Series
Curtis
Jared

The Dead Heat Ranch Series
Boots Optional
Betting on Grace
Overnight Love

By Nicole Edwards (cont.)

The Devil's Bend Series

Chasing Dreams
Vanishing Dreams

The Devil's Playground Series

Without Regret
Without Restraint

The Office Intrigue Series

Office Intrigue
Intrigued Out of the Office
Their Rebellious Submissive

The Pier 70 Series

Reckless
Fearless
Speechless
Harmless

The Sniper 1 Security Series

Wait for Morning
Never Say Never
Tomorrow's Too Late

The Southern Boy Mafia Series

Beautifully Brutal
Beautifully Loyal

Standalone Novels

A Million Tiny Pieces
Inked on Paper

Writing as Timberlyn Scott

Unhinged
Unraveling
Chaos

Naughty Holiday Editions

2015
2016

Overnight Love

A DEAD HEAT RANCH NOVELLA

Nicole Edwards

SL Independent Publishing, LLC
PO Box 806
Hutto, Texas 78634
www.**slipublishing**.com

ISBN: 978-1-939786-37-1 (ebook)
ISBN: 978-1-939786-38-8 (print)

Cover Images by: © Steve Everts | 123rf.com
Cover Design by: Nicole Edwards Limited
Editing by: Blue Otter Editing **www.blueotterediting.com**

Dear reader,

Overnight Love, although it does tie into my Dead Heat Ranch series, was written to be a standalone novella about Lucas Burch and Mackenzie Catlay. This is a contemporary, sweet love story that I hope you enjoy.

Nicole Edwards

Chapter One

ackenzie Catlay never imagined in all her life that she'd be walking into a backwoods, redneck, country bar to meet a man. Well, not like this, anyway.

A blind date.

Blind. Freaking. Date.

What had her life come to?

"What could it hurt, Kenzie?" her mother had asked the last time she'd come to visit, two weeks ago. They'd been sitting on Kenzie's back porch with the propane heater blasting, drinking wine and talking about what it had been like for her mother growing up in that very house and reminiscing about the times Kenzie had visited her grandparents there.

Between the two of them, they'd finished off two bottles of wine, and that was the first mistake Kenzie had made that night. The second had been turning on her computer.

At first, Kenzie had shunned the idea that her mother had easily planted in her mind. Laughed at it, even. But then, after perusing the Internet, she'd given in to the curiosity that had plagued her.

Her mother had mentioned a website that one of her friends had been raving about just a few weeks before. Until that moment, Kenzie had never considered trying to meet anyone, much less trying to find love, online. At twenty-six, she was content being alone, living in her grandparents' old ranch house, sharing her bed with her cat, and not having to answer to anyone. Yep, no issues whatsoever.

Or so she'd told herself.

Okay, so maybe that wasn't entirely true.

Until recently, she'd had a relatively busy dating life. It wasn't until she'd uprooted her life eight months ago and moved to the small town where her mother had grown up that she'd started enjoying the solitude that came with being single. Apparently, too much time by herself, spent only with the company of her cat, Jasper, or the occasional visit from her mother, had been her downfall, and Kenzie had given in to her curiosity, pulling up the website.

Just to look, she'd told herself.

"And you're here, why?" Kenzie ridiculed herself aloud as she made her way to the front door of the small bar, the rough gravel lot causing her to wobble in her three-inch heels a time or two, but thankfully, she didn't end up on her ass.

When Kenzie opened the door, cigarette smoke and the dull drone of conversation drifted out. Taking a step inside, she tried not to draw the attention of the people who were standing around, talking and laughing and having a good time. Although plenty of eyes slid her way, no one seemed to care that she was there. She wasn't sure whether that was a good thing or a bad thing.

The place was rustic, if that was the right word. Wood walls, wood floor, some animal heads and beer signs decorating the space, but mostly it was filled with men and women sharing conversation, a few dancing to the slow country tune playing on the jukebox.

A far cry from the bars Kenzie was used to visiting back in Houston.

"What can I getcha, honey?"

Kenzie glanced at the big-haired woman who was currently smacking gum and smiling like she knew a secret that Kenzie didn't.

She probably did.

These days, Kenzie felt out of the loop wherever she went, whether it was the grocery store or the bank. According to her mother, people in small towns prided themselves on knowing everyone, and until Kenzie made an effort to get to know people there, she was going to look like an outsider.

I'm here now, she thought to herself.

"Bud Light," Kenzie told the bartender, mentioning the first thing that came to mind. Since she didn't drink beer, she figured it didn't really matter what the label said. She'd merely be using it as a prop. Her drink of choice would've been a nice glass of wine, maybe a shot of something stronger, but definitely not beer. Considering she was meeting a man she'd only talked to on the Internet over the course of a week, keeping all her wits about her was the most important thing, as far as she was concerned. So, the beer was just an accessory. Something to say that she belonged there, when, in truth, based on the people standing around, she knew otherwise.

Amongst the cowboys in their western gear and the women in their rhinestone-encrusted outfits, Kenzie knew she looked out of place. She'd put on her favorite little black dress at the last minute, not wanting to spend more time than necessary digging through the boxes she had yet to unpack. The ones that contained her nice clothes, the outfits she'd worn when she'd had an active social life and not spending most of her time doing little more than take care of a few cows, a couple of horses, and a handful of chickens. Something she still had no idea how to do. Not well, anyway. Then again, that was why she still had Ralph, the ranch hand who'd been with her grandparents for longer than Kenzie could remember.

Nope, her black dress and killer heels stood out like a neon sign. This was a redneck bar, and Kenzie was a big-city transplant who was having a hard time fitting in no matter what she did.

Ever since moving to Embers Ridge, she'd settled on being a loner, hanging out at home with her cat and her livestock. Considering that the only reason she'd moved there was because her grandfather had left his small ranch to her when he'd passed away nine months ago, she wasn't surprised. The only human contact she'd had recently were the sporadic phone calls to a few of her friends in Houston, her mother's frequent visits, her late-night chats with her cat, and a couple of brief conversations with a guy named Joe. On the Internet.

"Here ya go, honey," the woman said as she set the bottle on the scarred bar top in front of Kenzie. "Haven't seen you 'round these parts."

Kenzie shook her head. "I'm not from around here."

"Couldn't tell," the other woman said facetiously, a wide smile on her bright red lips. "Name's Marla. Just holler if you need anything else."

Kenzie nodded, reaching for the bottle and pulling it closer to her. Glancing around the room, she tried to figure out whether or not her date had already arrived. Maybe he was hiding out so he could check her out first. She'd thought about doing that, arriving half an hour early so she could try and spy on him first, except she'd chickened out before she'd ever stepped out her front door.

It was actually a wonder she was there at all, but her conscience had gotten the best of her. She didn't want to stand Joe up. He'd been nice the few times they'd chatted online.

Neither of them had shared pictures of themselves, mainly because Kenzie hadn't been comfortable. It wasn't like there was any way to prove that he was who he said he was by a picture anyway. For whatever reason, she'd thought that meeting in person, in a public place, would be the way to go.

Crazy, she knew.

Yet here she was, and it looked like maybe she was the one who'd been stood up.

"Anyone sittin' here?"

Kenzie glanced up to look at the man who owned the smooth, rich voice. He was wearing a black Stetson and a navy blue button-down shirt, the sleeves rolled up to show thick, tanned forearms covered in crisp, dark hair. Thanks to the black Stetson resting on his head, she couldn't see his face. At least nothing other than chiseled cheekbones, lips that weren't smiling, and a five-o'clock shadow on his stubbornly set jaw.

He was handsome, she could tell that much. She just wished she could see his eyes.

"Not yet," she said absently, shifting on her stool to allow the man room to sit.

There was no way that this guy was Joe; even she knew that much. She just didn't get that lucky.

This guy didn't look like he needed to resort to an Internet dating site to meet women. Hell, for all she knew, he was married. As she reached for her beer, pretending to have a reason to be there, she glanced down at his hands when he set them on the wooden top. Nope. No ring.

Good sign.

No. Wait. That was not a good sign. That wasn't a sign at all. Kenzie wasn't there to meet a cowboy. She had no interest in cowboys, and this guy … he was all cowboy.

Not wanting to disturb him, she glanced in the mirror above the bar, searching the room for someone who might possibly be her date.

"Hey, Lucas," Marla greeted the man now sitting to her left.

Kenzie noticed Marla hadn't asked him what he wanted. Instead, she offered him a big grin as she slid over a short glass with amber liquid and ice.

"Hey, Marla. You're lookin' good tonight, honey," he said, that rich baritone of his making the hair on the back of Kenzie's neck stand up and take notice.

"You sweet-talkin' devil, you. Don't let Carl hear you say that."

"I wouldn't dream of it," Lucas replied with a gruff, far-too-sexy chuckle. "Wouldn't want your ol' man scalpin' me."

Kenzie found herself watching the cowboy in the mirror. He was tall, probably over six feet. Even sitting down, he made her feel significantly smaller by comparison, and that was saying something since Kenzie was tall herself. He was handsome, what she could see of him, anyway. For someone who was not her type. As she studied the angles of his face, the fullness of his lips, Kenzie tried to pretend to be looking elsewhere. When their eyes met in the mirror, she knew she'd been busted. The slight tilt of his lips was proof.

"Whose heart you gonna break tonight, darlin'?" Lucas asked, his eyes moving away from hers and down to the drink in front of him.

"Excuse me?" Kenzie wasn't sure whether he was talking to her or not, but there wasn't anyone else around, so she figured he might be.

"Nothin'. Ignore me," he said gruffly.

Kenzie nodded her head before taking a sip of her beer.

Yuck.

God, that tasted like shit.

A ruckus near the door had Kenzie turning on her stool, her back to Lucas. A man was walking in, and he looked as though he'd already tied one on. He was staggering and grabbing hold of anything he could reach just to keep himself upright, including an unlucky blonde standing near the door.

"Hey, girlie. You Mackenzie?" he asked one of the women he wrapped his arms around.

"Oh, God," Kenzie muttered.

"Know him?" Lucas asked.

Kenzie could feel the heat of Lucas's body against her back, causing a chill to race down her spine.

"I hope not," she answered honestly, glancing behind her to see that the good-looking cowboy was staring over her shoulder.

"Are *you* Mackenzie?" the drunk guy asked the next woman he encountered.

The way he stretched her name into way too many syllables made Kenzie cringe.

"I take it you're Mackenzie?" Lucas stated. His smoky voice, mixed with the warmth of his breath on her neck, was not doing her any favors.

"Can I lie and say no?" she asked frankly.

Lucas chuckled, but then his body heat left her as he turned back around to face the bar.

Crap.

What was she supposed to do about this guy? The drunk one. If he was, in fact, her date, which, unfortunately, she was pretty sure he was, there was no way this was going to go well. Joe something or other, who lived in Austin, sold real estate, and drove a Porsche that he prized more than anything — or so he'd told her online — was rip-roaring drunk. She obviously couldn't have a conversation with him. He could hardly stand up, much less talk.

Another woman shoved him off, and then a couple of guys moved him along until the man she assumed was Joe stumbled over to the bar. He planted himself on the barstool closest to Kenzie, and she suddenly wished she could click her heels together and disappear.

"Hey!" he hollered at Marla.

Marla shot a glare down toward his end of the bar, but she didn't move to serve him.

Kenzie turned back around and faced the wall lined with bottles, tipping her beer to her lips. Maybe if she didn't look at him, he wouldn't see her. God, she hoped he didn't see her.

"Hey! Can I get a beer down here?" Joe yelled at Marla again.

This time Lucas growled. The deep rumble coming from his chest had Kenzie jerking her head to look at him.

"I suggest you send him on his way before he gets himself hurt," Lucas said beneath his breath, his attention on the glass with the amber liquid sitting in front of him, his Stetson casting his ruggedly handsome face in shadow. "We practice these things called manners 'round these parts."

"He's not mine to deal with," Kenzie said defensively, trying not to move her lips too much, not wanting to draw Joe's attention to her.

"Are *you* Mackenzie?" Joe finally asked, and Kenzie glanced over at him. Yep, he was talking to her.

Crap.

She'd never been a good liar. And really, what good would it do to pretend she wasn't the date he'd come to meet? It wasn't like her night was going to get any better either way.

Chapter Two

Lucas Burch didn't want to pay attention to the blonde beauty sitting beside him, but from the moment he'd laid eyes on her, he hadn't been able to look away. When their gazes had met in the mirror above the bar, he'd feared she'd seen his interest written across his face.

He wasn't interested.

No damn way.

At thirty-eight years old, he had no use for women in his life, not even for one night. Especially not the young woman in the sexy black dress. Not after the number that'd been done on him by the woman whose name he refused to speak. The woman he'd spent the last thirteen years with. The same one who'd left him high and dry when she'd traded him in for a younger version.

But no matter how many times he told himself to get up and just go home, his legs weren't listening to the instruction. Stopping in to grab a drink had seemed like a good idea, right up to the point he'd come in and seen her. And now his ass was planted on the barstool right next to the blonde in the slinky black dress, and for the first time in months, his body was insisting that he get to know her a little better.

She couldn't have stood out more if she'd been wearing a flashing sign on her head. Hell, Lucas wasn't sure he'd ever seen a woman dressed like that come into the place he considered his second home, aptly named Marla's Bar after the owner, Marla White. Never.

Not that he had anything against that damn dress. The black number clung to every delicious curve, accentuating her narrow waist and rounded ass. And her legs... Son of a bitch, her legs had to be at least a mile long. He could imagine them wrapped around his hips while he...

No, you can't, dumbass.

Lucas shook his head, trying to dislodge the image. His body was already responding, and he knew there wasn't enough alcohol in the place to soothe him if he let his lust get the best of him.

It'd been six damn months since he'd been with any woman. Period.

Lucas sipped his scotch, pretending that Makenzie wasn't sitting next to him and that her sweet perfume wasn't making his head spin. It was subtle, not quite what he expected from the likes of her.

When the drunk bastard at the end of the bar asked whether she was Mackenzie, Lucas shifted his head ever so slightly so he could look at her.

Her eyes widened, and he knew without a doubt she wished she wasn't.

What surprised him was the numerous expressions that crossed her pretty face. She wasn't going to lie to the man, and Lucas wondered why that was. They clearly didn't know each other. Hell, the guy didn't even know what she looked like. Either that or he was just that drunk and had confused every woman, no matter their hair color, for the woman sitting at the bar.

"Blind date?" Lucas asked, keeping his voice low enough that only she could hear.

"Unfortunately," Makenzie said just as softly.

"So, *are* you Mackenzie or what?" the guy asked her again, his words slurred.

"I ... uh..."

"You ready to get out of here, love?" Lucas asked, pushing to his feet and placing his hand on Mackenzie's back, leaning down until his nose was inches from her neck. Despite the fact that he was a grown man and knew better, he inhaled the fresh scent of her hair.

She smelled like strawberries.

Lord, help him.

Mackenzie turned her head slightly, but then Lucas was pressing his nose against the soft skin of her neck, his lips brushing her shoulder. He felt a tremor run through her, and an answering one shot through him.

He should've pulled away. It would've been the noble thing to do, but by then, his cock was rock-fucking-hard, and he wasn't sure he was capable of moving away. Ever.

"Hey! Bartender! I'd like a beer down here," the drunk bastard exclaimed.

"Yes. Yes, I am ready to go," Mackenzie said firmly, twisting on her stool until she was facing Lucas directly.

Holding out his hand, Lucas helped her down. The soft skin of her fingers brushing against his had his breath catching momentarily.

And then their eyes met for the first time without the mirror. He found himself lost in her chocolate-brown gaze, unable to look away although he knew he should.

There was no doubt in his mind that his dry spell was about to end. It didn't matter that he'd sworn off women for eternity, Lucas knew that if this woman gave him the slightest signal that she'd go home with him, he was a goner.

Catching a glimpse of Marla making her way down to the end of the bar, Lucas knew it was time to hightail it out of Dodge. He grabbed his wallet from his back pocket, pulled out two twenties, and slapped them on the bar. Marla noticed the movement and nodded at him.

"Come on," he encouraged Mackenzie, linking his fingers with hers and pulling her behind him as he made a beeline for the door. He snagged his jacket from the rack on the wall on the way out, sliding it over his arm.

Once they were outside, the cool January breeze caressed his overheated skin, and Lucas thought for a minute that he might be able to regain his equilibrium.

"Th-thank you," Mackenzie said, wrapping her arms around her body as she followed him down the steps and into the parking lot.

"For?" he asked, confused.

"For saving me."

"You do that often?" he asked, nodding his head toward the bar.

"What?"

"Blind dates?"

She laughed, the throaty sound not helping the heat in his veins to dissipate.

"No, I don't. First *and* last time."

Lucas nodded. He needed to get away from her, and the only way to do that was to send her on her way. "Where's your car?"

Mackenzie spun around slowly, her body trembling from the chill in the air. "Over there."

She was pointing to the side of the building. The same area where he'd parked his truck, so he placed his hand on the small of her back and guided her around the building. It was dark, the single light in the parking lot not reaching the far side of the building. Without thinking, Lucas pulled her against him, keeping his hand firmly on her hip while he navigated her past the parking stones and the potholes, not wanting to see her fall in those sexy fucking heels.

Or at least that was his excuse.

"You okay to drive home?" he asked when she stopped behind a nondescript little Ford Focus.

"Uhh..."

She was watching him intently, her pretty brown eyes roaming over his face. He waited for her to answer, fighting the grin.

"I didn't have anything to drink," she admitted, tearing her gaze away.

Lucas suddenly felt bereft without the intensity of her gaze on him. Not thinking, he lifted his hand and placed his finger beneath her chin, tilting her head so that she would look at him again.

Mackenzie was tall, probably close to six foot with the heels, which put her almost eye level with him. At six three, Lucas didn't often encounter women who were close to his height, and he decided that he liked the fact that she was.

Their eyes met, locked. The only time he looked away was when his gaze slid down her face to hover on her sweet, pouty lips.

He suddenly had the urge to taste her.

But he was a gentleman, and gentlemen damn sure didn't rescue damsels in distress just to make out with them in the parking lot of a seedy little backwoods bar. Not to mention, he wasn't twenty-five.

Or interested.

Right. Not interested. Keep telling yourself that.

For a brief, mind-numbing second, Lucas thought Mackenzie was going to kiss *him*, and for the first time in as long as he could remember, he wasn't flooded with outrage at the thought of taking a woman to bed and waking up beside her the next morning.

But then everything went to shit.

"Hey!" the drunken voice sounded from a few feet away, and Lucas turned to see the asshole from the bar standing behind him. "Where're you goin'?"

"Can I help you?" Lucas asked sternly, turning and instinctively stepping in front of Mackenzie.

"That's my date," the guy yelled.

"*That?*" Lucas asked, confused.

"Yeah," he slurred. "That woman."

"*That woman* has a name," Lucas growled, suddenly pissed that a guy like this could end up with a woman like Mackenzie in the first place.

You don't know her, dumbass.

Lucas ignored the annoying voice in his head, doing his best to focus on the situation at hand.

"Her name is Mackenzie."

Mackenzie's firm hand gripped Lucas's arm, pulling his attention to her as she stepped around to his side. "It's okay," she said, her voice soft. "He really is my problem."

"How do you figure?" Lucas questioned, more confused than ever.

What the hell was it with these people?

"I invited him here."

"Did you ask him to get shit-faced drunk before he came?" Lucas countered.

"Well, no, but—"

Maybe it was the fact that he hadn't been with a woman in seven months, just a couple of months after his wife had left him, or just because he hadn't met a woman who made his body ache the way this one did in a long damn time, but whatever it was, Lucas did something he'd never done before.

Sliding his hand behind Mackenzie's neck, beneath the silky fall of her blonde hair, Lucas pulled her to him and brushed his lips against hers. When her hands came up and gripped his shirt, pulling him closer, not pushing him away, Lucas's good intentions snapped.

She smelled so damn good, her skin was so fucking soft, and her lips... She tasted like ambrosia.

Unable to resist, Lucas sealed his mouth with hers, thrusting his tongue inside, and was surprised to the tips of his boots when she kissed him back with as much, if not more, passion than he dished out.

Her soft, sexy moan nearly sent him to his knees.

That was until the drunk jackass came out of nowhere, pushing Lucas hard, which, in turn, sent Mackenzie to her knees on the gravel.

A red haze clouded his vision at the sight of Mackenzie on the ground, and before he could think better of it, Lucas turned and landed one punch to the drunk asshole's jaw, knocking him out cold.

"Are you okay?" Lucas asked, squatting down in front of her, sliding his hand over her knee. It was too dark for him to see, but her hiss told him that she wasn't okay.

"I'll be fine," she said, her voice shaky.

Helping her up, Lucas got her steady on her feet. "Give me a sec, would ya?"

Mackenzie nodded.

Realizing he couldn't just leave the asshole in the parking lot to sleep it off — although the idea had merit — Lucas made his way over to him, slapped him on the face a couple of times to rouse him. Finally, the guy's eyes opened.

"You asswipe. You fucking hit me."

"You're lucky that's all I did," Lucas grumbled as he yanked the guy to his feet. "Don't move," he instructed Mackenzie before pushing the guy back toward the front of the bar, intending to leave him inside, where he could become someone else's problem.

And that was exactly what he did.

Only, when he came back, Mackenzie and the little silver Ford Focus were gone.

And his night officially had gone to shit.

Chapter Three

"Damn it," Kenzie cursed as she hobbled into the house, trying her best not to bend her left knee. She had made the mistake of going out to the barn, wanting to make sure she had supplies in the event the weather got as bad as the weatherman had promised. Of course, had she listened to Ralph, she wouldn't have needed to check anything. The man had everything covered, which he'd adamantly told her. Twice.

She hadn't considered how painful the short trek would be.

After fleeing the parking lot incident at the bar two nights ago, she had come home to find that her little brush with the gravel had left her with a battered left knee, and even two days later, the damn thing wasn't doing much better. She didn't need a doctor, she knew that much; however, a little triple-antibiotic ointment and some Band-Aids probably wouldn't hurt. But she'd been putting that off because her first-aid kit was looking a little sparse these days. Apparently, it was time to give in and run into town, because the damn thing kept bleeding, and it was more irritating than anything else.

Glancing at the clock, she noticed it was after eight in the morning, which meant the small pharmacy in downtown Embers Ridge would be open. Figuring she could kill two birds with one stone, she made a quick phone call to the vet, letting them know she was going to come in to pick up an antibiotic for her cat, Jasper. She had learned last week that curiosity very well could kill a cat. Jasper, always having lived inside, had snuck out the door, and by the time Kenzie had found her two hours later, Jasper had managed to get a rather nasty cut on her paw, which had resulted in a quick trip to the vet. They had sent Kenzie and Jasper home with instructions to keep an eye on the cut. She had, but unfortunately, it wasn't getting better.

Twenty minutes later, Kenzie was pulling into the parking lot of the pharmacy after having stopped at the vet's office long enough to race inside and grab Jasper's medicine. There was a threat of more ice in the forecast, something that was relatively unheard of in this part of Texas, but this had been a freakishly cold winter so far. Unfortunately, Kenzie was wearing shorts, because putting anything else on was a recipe for disaster. Since her knee continued to bleed randomly and since she'd never bothered to buy any casual clothes when she'd moved to Embers Ridge, she wasn't fond of ruining what she did have. And now she had to get out of the car for the second time, which she truly wasn't looking forward to.

Pulling her heavy jacket tight to her body, she pushed open the door, fighting the frigid wind as she climbed out of her car and hobbled to the front door. By the time she was inside, she was freezing and shivering, cursing herself for being so stupid. Surely she had a pair of sweatpants that she could've parted with. This was ridiculous.

Making her way to the back of the store, Kenzie located the aisle with the bandages and antibiotic ointment. On her way to the front register, she detoured down the candy aisle, figuring she might as well grab something to curb the chocolate craving she'd been battling since the night of the parking lot incident. It was that or risk the possibility of going crazy. Or worse, having to get out in the cold once again just to indulge herself when she finally did give in. Which she undoubtedly would.

Holding her items close to her chest, Kenzie glanced down as she made her way to the front, trying to keep the small box of bandages from slipping from her hands when she bumped into something big and … hard.

"Careful, girl." The deep, rough voice was so familiar her body ignited instantly, even though she was about to have another collision course with the ground. If it hadn't been for the strong arms that enveloped her, she would've done just that.

Somehow she managed to hold on to her items, even as she looked up into those mesmerizing green eyes that had haunted her dreams for the last two nights. "Lucas."

"We're gonna have to stop meetin' like this, darlin'," he said, his rumbling tone doing little to curb the heat that had infused her body.

At least she wasn't cold anymore.

"Are you…?" Lucas released her when she was steady on her feet as he glanced down at her legs. "Why the hell are you wearin' shorts?" he asked.

All of the heat that had been traveling through her body made a sudden detour right to her face. "I…" Hell, she didn't even know how to answer that.

And then Lucas was squatting down in front of her, his big, rough hand wrapping behind her left knee. The sensation was absurdly sensual, although she knew he was just looking at her scrape. "Is this from the other night?"

"Yeah," she managed to mutter, sounding breathless and silly. "No big deal. Just came in to grab some Band-Aids."

"Two days later," Lucas said as he rose to his feet.

"Yeah," Kenzie replied, a little frustrated at his tone. "Sorry I wasn't watchin' where I was goin'." Feeling a little embarrassed, both at her less-than-graceful encounter with Lucas and with her lack of clothing, she knew it was time to take her leave.

"My fault," Lucas said, his gaze meeting hers.

Unsure what to say to that, Kenzie forced a smile and then nodded as she stepped around him toward the register. The young woman was staring at the two of them like they'd lost their minds. Considering there were no other customers in the store, the girl probably found their brief interaction amusing, which didn't help Kenzie's embarrassment.

After paying for her items, she slipped her purse back on her arm, and then the small plastic bag, as she headed for the door. Before she could push it open, a big arm reached around her, doing it for her. She didn't have to look back to know who it was, and she wondered for a brief moment whether the universe was out to get her. Wasn't it bad enough that she was hobbling along with blood staining her leg? She probably looked like she'd crawled out of a hole somewhere.

"Thank you," she said as she stepped out into the frosty morning air, gripping her jacket as tightly as she could.

When she reached her car, that same arm came around and opened her door for her. This time Kenzie did turn around, only to find Lucas was standing directly behind her, his eyes locking with hers instantly.

"So you live here?" he asked quickly.

Sighing, she knew she couldn't be rude. After all, he was just being a gentleman. And it hadn't been entirely his fault what had happened the other night. The kiss that had rocked her world. The kiss she hadn't been able to stop thinking about. Since she'd been the one on the other side of that kiss, fusing her mouth with his, she was partially to blame, as well.

Don't look at his mouth. Don't look at his mouth.

Oh, damn. She was looking at his mouth.

"Darlin', keep lookin' at me like that and I'm gonna kiss you again."

The rich, dark rumble of his voice caressed her like a physical touch, and she was suddenly grateful that she could sit down. Which she did, breaking the hold he had on her and sliding into her car.

"You didn't answer my question," Lucas said, his hand planted on the top of the open car door.

What question?

His gruff chuckle made her insides tremble, and she knew she needed to get the hell out of there before she did something stupid. Like invite him to her house.

"I live off 198," she said.

"The old Catlay place?"

"That'd be the one. My grandfather left it to me."

Lucas's eyes softened. "I'm sorry for your loss. Glenn was a good man."

Unsure what to say to that, Kenzie muttered a thank you before pulling her legs into the car and turning the key. She was freezing. "I need to get home," she finally said when it was apparent he wasn't going to leave. "Looks like we might get some ice."

The sky had darkened, and there were small droplets of water already forming on her windshield, which meant if she didn't hurry, she wasn't going to beat the storm, and she knew without a doubt that her little Ford wasn't going to do well on the icy roads. She'd been meaning to get the tires changed, but since she hadn't been driving much, she'd put it off.

"Be careful," Lucas said as he took a step back and then closed her door for her.

Kenzie fought the urge to look up at him one more time before she put the car in reverse and backed out of the small space.

And as she drove out of the parking lot, as more water began to dot her windshield, she suddenly wished she had a reason to invite Lucas back to her place.

Chapter Four

Lucas made his way back inside the pharmacy when Mackenzie's car pulled out of the parking lot. He'd stopped in to grab a few things, not wanting to make a trip into the neighboring town because of the weather, but after running into her — literally — he had forgotten just what it was that he needed.

Fifteen minutes later, he'd grabbed a can of stew and a package of crackers, figuring that would be the extent of dinner for the night. Well, that and maybe a fifth of whiskey. That was what he was really wanting, something to dull the thoughts that had been plaguing him for the last two days. The ones that had started about the same time that his lips had touched Mackenzie's in that damn parking lot of the bar. Not that he was getting the whiskey at the local pharmacy. Lucky for him, he had that at home.

As he made his way to the register, he thought about Mackenzie's knee. It wasn't bad, just a little scrape, but the injury appeared to be in just the right place — the bend of her knee — to keep it from healing quickly. It didn't sit well with him that she'd gotten that damn scratch because of him, either.

"Hey, Lucas," Tracey greeted when he set his items on the counter.

"Hey, Trace. You headin' home soon?" he asked as he glanced out the door. "Weather's gettin' bad."

"Yes, sir. After I ring you up, I'm headin' out."

"Good girl. Tell your dad I said hello," Lucas said after he paid and took the plastic sack from the counter.

"I'll do it."

Tracey followed Lucas to the door, and once he was outside, he heard the telltale click of the deadbolt on the door. He rushed to his truck just as the sleet got heavier, coating his hair and his face with little ice pellets.

"Shit."

Lucas knew that the road back to his place was going to be hell to drive on. Even in the four-wheel-drive truck, he was going to have to navigate slowly or he was going to end up in a ditch.

His thoughts immediately drifted to Mackenzie. He'd seen her drive out of the parking lot, and he'd noticed when her back tires had lost traction as she'd turned onto the main road. Her tires were bald, which meant her trek home was probably going to be trickier than his.

"You shouldn't be worried about her, dumbass," Lucas grumbled aloud as he turned the key in the ignition and put the truck in gear. Backing out of the parking spot, he watched as the lights inside the pharmacy went out.

Ten minutes later, Lucas was pulling to a stop behind the familiar silver Ford Focus that'd left the pharmacy a good fifteen minutes before him, sitting on the side of the road, nose first in a ditch. It was still daylight, but with the cloud cover, it was gloomy, and with the heavy sleet, it was difficult to make out the car completely, but he knew without a doubt that it was Mackenzie.

"Should've known," he huffed as he climbed out of his truck, pulling his jacket closed. He made his way around the car and tapped on the driver's window.

"Are you stalking me?" Mackenzie asked with a grin as she lowered the window.

Lucas laughed; he couldn't help himself. Truthfully, he'd expected her to be a wreck, sitting in her car, waiting for someone to come save her. He wouldn't have been surprised if she'd been crying, either. That was what most women he knew would've been doing. They certainly wouldn't be smiling.

"Chocolate?" she asked, holding up a candy bar.

And they definitely wouldn't be offering him chocolate.

"Get out, woman," he grumbled, reaching for the handle and pulling her door open.

"Pushy, aren't ya?" she asked, chuckling.

"Did you hit your head or somethin'?" Lucas asked, reaching for Mackenzie's arm and helping her out of the car. Once she was upright, he closed the car door, still keeping a firm grip on her arm so that she didn't fall.

"No, why?"

"'Cause you're awful damn happy for a woman who just drove her car into a ditch."

"First of all, I didn't drive it there, it went there on its own."

"And that's funny?" Lucas asked as he led her over to the passenger side of his truck.

"Not at all. But I figure bein' upset won't change my luck, so I might as well smile."

Well, there you had it.

"Oh, wait. I need my Band-Aids," Mackenzie called out just as Lucas was about to close the truck door, sealing her inside.

He nodded and made his way back to her car, retrieving the pharmacy bag, locking the car doors, and returning to his truck.

Thankfully, the truck heater was on full blast, because it was colder than a well digger's ass.

"You live out here?" Mackenzie asked when he got settled behind the wheel.

"The Double B," Lucas murmured, putting the truck in gear.

"Well, thanks for pickin' me up," Mackenzie said as he pulled back onto the road, his back tires losing traction once or twice.

"That's what neighbors do," he said, doing his best not to look over at her.

The heater was blasting, but it didn't do a damn thing to mask the scent of her perfume. That same sweet scent from the other night at the bar that had left him light-headed.

Fortunately, Mackenzie remained silent for the few minutes it took him to drive her to her front door. And he probably would've gotten away easily if it hadn't been for his stupid-ass mouth deciding to open up and say something ... well, something stupid.

"Why'd you run off the other night?"

Mackenzie's hand was on the door handle, but she stopped, turning to look at him, her eyes wide.

Yep, he was a dumbass.

"I ... uh..."

"Never mind," Lucas grumbled, knowing he should've just kept his mouth shut. The fact that he'd told her to stay put while he had helped that drunk asshole back into the bar so someone could get him home safely, only for Lucas to return and find her gone, should've been the only answer he needed.

"I should've thanked you," Mackenzie said, turning to face him more fully as she held her plastic sack of supplies close to her chest. He had a hard time keeping his eyes on her face when her long legs peeked out from beneath her coat. He still couldn't believe the woman was wearing shorts when the temperature was hovering right at the freezing mark.

"Not necessary," Lucas told her, keeping his tone even as he pulled his eyes away from her and stared out the front windshield.

She was silent for a moment, and he thought she was going to leave it at that, but then she had to go and open her mouth again. "You wanna come in for some coffee?"

Lucas had no idea what the hell he was thinking, but for a brief moment, he actually considered the offer. Luckily, before he did something stupid like accept, he came to his senses.

"Gotta get back before the roads get too bad."

"Oh, okay."

Lucas met her gaze and silently scolded himself for it. She was so damn beautiful, even with her hair piled on top of her head and not a lick of makeup on her face. She actually looked better than she had the other night in that sexy black dress and those high heels that'd made her legs look ten miles long.

"Well, thanks again."

"Yup."

Mackenzie climbed out of the truck, shutting the door with a gentle click before turning to the front porch. She turned back once, and Lucas knew he should've looked away, but he couldn't help himself. When she waved at him, he kept his hands on the steering wheel. No sense in making her think he was friendly, because he wasn't.

And then, just when he thought he was going to get safely back home without having to deal with the only woman who'd caught his attention in recent months, Mackenzie had to go and slip.

"Son of a bitch," he growled, turning off the engine and grabbing the keys before jumping out of the truck and trudging over to her, slipping and sliding on the ice that was forming faster than he had expected. "You okay?" he asked, going to his knee to put his arms around her and help her to her feet.

Her knee was bleeding again, more than it had been before. Reckoning he'd already stepped out of the frying pan and into the fire by talking to her in the first place, Lucas figured what the hell. Sliding his hands beneath her, he lifted her into his arms, holding her close to his chest. When she wrapped her arms around his neck, his senses flooded with the sweet scent of strawberries, he knew he was in deep, deep shit.

Chapter Five

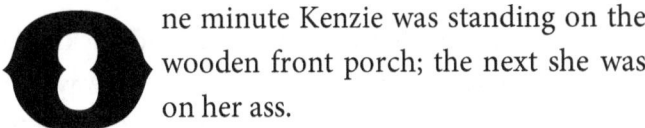ne minute Kenzie was standing on the wooden front porch; the next she was on her ass.

She might've been able to handle it if she'd been the only one to see her less-than-graceful fall to the ground, but of course, just as her luck would have it, Lucas had witnessed the whole thing. And now she was in his arms, inhaling that sexy, musky scent that she remembered from the other night. She doubted it was cologne. Aftershave, maybe. Regardless, he smelled fantastic.

His jacket was cold, but his neck was warm as she wrapped her arm around him, praying he wouldn't drop her. She wasn't a wisp of a thing, and well, he wasn't young. Kenzie wasn't sure how old he was, but she figured his late thirties, although he looked even older than that. He'd certainly done some hard living at some point in his life.

"I can walk," she assured him when he snagged her keys from her hand and inserted them into the front door.

"I'm beginnin' to question whether that's true," he mumbled, making her grin.

Why she was smiling, she had no idea. She liked Lucas. The way he smelled, the gruff rumble of his voice, the way he looked at her as though he'd never met anyone like her. All of those things, not to mention the memory of his lips on hers, had plagued her for the last couple of days.

And suddenly here he was.

He carried her over the threshold, kicking her front door closed with his boot before making his way through the house. Kenzie found it amusing that he didn't think to ask directions; instead, Lucas made a couple of wrong turns before he found the kitchen. She didn't bother to tell him that there had been a straight path from the front door. It was more interesting this way.

When he set her on the counter, she was reluctant to let go of him. Not because she feared that she would fall to the floor, more because she didn't want to let go.

He released her slowly, and Kenzie allowed her hand to slide over his slightly rough cheek. The dark hair lining his angular jaw scraped against her fingers, sending a chill across her skin. Lucas's gaze settled on her face, their eyes meeting, but he didn't move away. This was what she'd dreamed about, what she had craved since the first and only time he had pressed his lips to hers.

Lucas's eyes traveled down to her mouth, lingering there, and Kenzie found herself holding her breath, willing him to kiss her.

"We better get you patched up," Lucas whispered roughly.

They were so close Kenzie could feel his breath against her lips, and for a second, she considered kissing him, making that first move that would lead exactly where she wanted it to.

It'd been a long time for her.

But Lucas pulled away, shaking his head as though he was trying to make sense of the situation.

"I'm good," Kenzie finally said, realizing there wasn't going to be a heated make-out session in her kitchen, no matter how much she wished it. "I can take care of it. Sorry about making you come out here."

Right then, Jasper decided to join the conversation, hopping up onto the counter beside Kenzie and staring at the sexy stranger. Jasper offered a quick meow.

"Lucas, meet Jasper. Jasper, meet Lucas," Kenzie said, running her hand down Jasper's soft gray fur.

Lucas didn't respond. Not to her earlier statement and not to her introduction to the cat. At first, he just stood there, glancing between her and Jasper, and at first, Kenzie thought he was just going to turn and leave, but then, faster than her brain could process, Lucas was standing in front of her, his hand sliding behind her head, pulling her to him. Their mouths collided. Lips, teeth, tongue. The kiss was gloriously brutal but so damn sweet at the same time.

Kenzie exhaled on a moan, sliding her hands up behind his head and linking her fingers in the soft strands of his dark hair peeking out from beneath his hat. She didn't want to let him go, and she definitely couldn't explain her reaction to him. She'd never been the spontaneous sort. Never had a one-night stand. Never made out with a man whose last name she didn't know. But here she was, throwing caution to the wind, and she couldn't even convince herself it was a bad idea.

Jasper meowed loudly, making Kenzie smile against Lucas's mouth.

"Fuck," Lucas growled, pulling back but not releasing her. His fingers were twined in her hair; he was cupping her head, holding her so that she had to look at him. "What're you doin' to me?"

"I don't know," she admitted softly. "But whatever it is … I feel it, too."

Lucas's green eyes widened, and then he was backing up, his hands falling to his sides as he stared at her as though she'd sprouted a third eyeball.

Clearly she'd said the wrong thing.

"I shouldn't be here," he admitted, turning away from her and thrusting his hands into his coat pockets.

"Then go," she said quickly, mortified that he was turning this around on her. Sure, she'd willingly kissed him, but he acted as though she had lured him there.

Lucas turned around, meeting her gaze once more. She could see the heat still lingering in the emerald depths, feel the tension radiating from his big body, but for the life of her, she had no idea what he was thinking.

"You gonna be okay?" he asked, nodding toward her knee.

Kenzie glanced down at her leg. The bleeding had stopped, but her leg needed to be cleaned. "I'm gonna be perfectly fine," she told him matter-of-factly, forcing a smile. "Thanks again. I'll call a tow truck to get my car."

Lucas nodded his head, and then he looked toward the front door.

God, what had she possibly done that made this man want to run out the door?

The thought pissed her off, and she hopped down off the counter and motioned toward the living room, signaling for the exit. Jasper jumped down as well, circling her legs. "I'll walk you out."

Lucas looked at her again, and Kenzie was pretty sure that was confusion reflecting back at her, but she didn't know for sure. Clearly he'd figured it out, because he started walking, making it all the way to the front door before he stopped. He pivoted slowly around to look at her, and Kenzie held her breath.

"I can't do this."

Kenzie narrowed her eyes, trying to understand what he was talking about. "I didn't ask you to do anything," she retorted, suddenly consumed by a slow, burning anger that flooded her bloodstream.

"You didn't have to," he answered.

"Look, Lucas—" Kenzie's retort was cut off when Lucas grabbed her again, pulling her against him. Instinct kicked in, and she threw her arms around his neck, meeting his lips when he bent to kiss her.

A frenzy of energy kicked up around them, heating the room to unbearable levels. Before she knew it, Lucas lifted her and turned, pressing her back into the door. Wrapping her legs around his waist, she thrust her tongue against him, pressing her breasts against the hard plane of his chest, trying to get closer, although his coat and hers made it damn near impossible to get close enough.

Spontaneous combustion.

That was what it felt like. At least to her. She was going to explode at any moment, and this man, this cowboy she didn't even know, was going to send her soaring into the ether. And she didn't want him to stop.

"What are we doing?" he asked, his lips lingering above hers when he finally pulled back.

"I don't know."

"Where is this headin'?" he asked, causing Kenzie to pull back so she could look in his eyes.

"The bedroom?"

Lucas's gruff chuckle vibrated through her, and Kenzie knew right then and there that she was going to do something she'd never done before.

And she couldn't bring herself to regret one single second.

Chapter Six

Lucas had no fucking idea what he was doing, but his brain had long ago stopped making his decisions for him. His dick was making all the calls right now, and the damn thing was yelling so loudly he couldn't hear anything else. Wanting this woman, desperate to drive himself inside her until she was screaming his name, begging for him to make her come, was the only thing he could think of at the moment.

And if that wasn't bad enough, the crazy woman had suggested that he take her to the bedroom.

"Second thoughts?" she asked, continuing to watch him as he held her firmly against the door, her long, trim legs wrapped around his waist.

"Hell, no," he ground out, slamming his mouth over hers once again, allowing her sweetness to shove away the anger and frustration that had filled him for so long.

She tasted like honey and sin mixed together. She was too damn sweet for the likes of him, but he couldn't resist her. However, he needed to know that they were on the same page here. He didn't want anything more than one night. If that. He just needed to get her out of his damn system, and he'd be out the door. He needed to ensure she understood that. Needed to know that she didn't expect anything more than a night of intense orgasms. He couldn't offer her anything else, but he knew without a doubt he could offer her that.

"One night," he mumbled against her mouth, trying to catch his breath as he released her soft lips.

"One night," she repeated.

"That's all I can give you," he explained, his eyes closing as she teased his lips with her soft tongue.

"That's all I need," she answered.

"Are you sure? You understand what I'm tellin' you, Mackenzie?"

"Call me Kenzie," she replied. "And I get it. One night. Nothing else. I'm not asking for a ring here, cowboy."

Shit.

Lucas laughed, hitching her up and tightening his grip on her as he turned. "Where's the bedroom?"

"That way," she whispered with a grin before sliding her tongue in his mouth once again.

Son of a bitch.

The woman was fire in his arms. Her desperate need to get him in the bedroom damn near rivaled his own.

What Lucas couldn't understand was why he was so damned hesitant to take her there. To toss her on the bed, strip off her clothes, and make love to her until the sun went down and then some more until the damn thing came back up. But something was niggling at him. That damn thing called his conscience. For whatever reason, he didn't want to hurt her. Emotionally. Didn't want to walk out the door in the morning and never see her again.

And that confused the fuck out of him, because he didn't even know her.

"Come on, cowboy," Kenzie said, nipping his bottom lip.

"I'm gettin' there, darlin'," he whispered, forcing his legs to carry him down the hallway. There were four doors, which meant he had a twenty-five percent chance of getting it right.

"Last one on the left," Kenzie stated, making his decision that much easier.

Pushing the door open with his foot, Lucas peered inside, noting the simple furnishings. A bed, dresser, nightstand. The woman was simple, he'd give her that. There wasn't a light on in the room, so it was difficult to make out anything other than the large pieces of furniture.

Not that he needed a light. Not for what they planned to do.

Putting her on her feet, Lucas didn't let go of Kenzie, fusing his lips to hers and cupping her face in his hands.

When she shrugged out of her jacket, tossing it onto the dresser behind him, Lucas sucked in a breath. And then, when she reached beneath his jacket for his shirt, pulling it from the waistband of his jeans, he held his breath. Her fingers found his skin, soft and cool against him, and he knew... He knew he'd waited too damn long for this. He'd purposely sealed himself off from the world, blocking everyone out because a woman had crushed his heart into a million pieces. Yet here he was, ready to jump into bed with a woman he hardly knew, a woman he feared, after just talking to her a few times, sharing a few blazing-hot kisses, could very possibly get under his skin.

"Lucas." Kenzie whispered his name as she pulled away from him. "I want this."

She sounded as though she were trying to reassure him, but what she didn't know was that he was trying to reassure himself. And it wasn't working.

As much as he wanted to be that guy, the one who could spend the afternoon fucking this incredibly beautiful woman into oblivion, he knew he'd hate himself tomorrow.

And possibly her, too.

"Fuck," he growled, pulling away from her and pacing in the opposite direction.

He still had his fucking coat on, damn it. What the hell was wrong with him?

Turning back to look at her, Lucas noticed her eyes were wide. "I'm sorry."

Kenzie's sweet mouth turned up in a slow grin as she stared back at him. Her charming giggle had his nerves settling.

"What's so damn funny?" he grumbled.

"You. Is it just me or are the roles a little reversed here?"

"Perhaps." He couldn't argue with her logic.

"You know what's even funnier?" she asked, still smiling.

Lucas cocked an eyebrow, waiting for her to enlighten him.

"I've never done this before."

"What? Sex?" *God, please don't let her be a virgin.* "Or a one-night stand?"

"The last one," she said sweetly, her eyes softening. "I didn't mean to attack you when you so kindly saved my butt."

"Darlin', trust me, I ain't complainin'."

"Come on," Kenzie said, reaching her hand out for him to take. "How 'bout that coffee?"

Unsure what he was supposed to say or do, Lucas took her hand and followed her into the kitchen. Shrugging out of his coat, he placed it over the back of a chair before sliding into the wooden seat. He watched her, the easy way she moved around her kitchen. He noticed she was limping, and that bothered him. He hated the fact that she'd been hurt, and maybe that was one of the reasons he was acting like a fucking pussy.

What thirty-eight-year-old man walked away from a woman like Kenzie? What the hell was he thinking? He could've been naked, buried balls deep in her by now, but instead he was in the kitchen, sitting at the table, waiting for her to make a pot of coffee. Yep, it was safe to say he was an idiot.

Once she had the pot brewing, she moved over to the island and retrieved the bag she'd brought from the pharmacy.

"Sit down," he urged her, taking the bag from her and dumping its contents on the table in front of him.

"Yes, sir."

"Put your foot on my leg," he instructed, moving his knee out so she could rest her leg on him.

A few minutes later, he had cleaned and doctored her scrape with the peroxide she'd pulled from the cabinet, then applied the ointment and bandaged her up.

"Good as new," he said.

Kenzie grinned and got to her feet. "Thank you."

A minute later, she returned to the table with two mugs. "Need cream or sugar?" she asked kindly.

"No. Despite my earlier actions, I'm not a fucking girl," he retorted without heat.

"No, I'd have to agree. You're certainly not a girl." The desire in her gaze made his dick throb. He was still hard, still aching, but he was doing his damnedest to ignore the damn thing.

It wasn't easy.

"So, tell me about yourself," Kenzie prompted, sliding into the chair across from him rather than taking the one beside him, where she'd been only moments ago.

"Not much to tell," he answered, immediately realizing his mistake.

There was plenty to tell. Especially to a woman he didn't know. One he surprisingly wanted to get to know a little better. Maybe then he could quit being a fucking pussy and take her to bed like he had planned half an hour ago.

Kenzie smiled, clearly realizing he'd dodged her question. "You grow up here?"

"Born and raised."

"You got a last name?"

"Burch."

"Nice to meet you, Lucas Burch." Her sweet smile did strange things to him. "Kenzie Catlay."

He didn't know what to say to that, so he sipped his coffee, keeping his eyes locked with hers. At least they knew each other's last name. It was a start.

"You knew my grandfather?" she asked, her eyebrow lifting slightly.

"I did. Glenn was good friends with my father." Lucas wasn't sure how he felt about that explanation. Realizing that his father was friends with her grandfather reflected the clear gap in their ages. But as much as he wanted to ask her how old she was, he held his tongue.

"My mother grew up here, too," Kenzie explained. "But she left when she was eighteen. She came back to visit, and I came and stayed quite a bit when I was young. Until my grandfather passed. I hadn't been back for a couple of years, though."

Lucas could see the sadness in her eyes, and he suddenly wanted to do whatever it would take to clear the clouds and bring back the sunshine that seemed to radiate from her, even on the dreariest of days.

"How old are you, Kenzie?" he asked point-blank.

"Isn't it rude to ask a lady that question?" she retorted instantly, grinning once more.

"Probably." He knew the answer was more of a yes, but he still wanted to know.

"How old are you?" she countered.

"Old enough to be your father," he rattled, looking down at the mug in front of him.

Kenzie laughed, the sweet sound filling the kitchen and causing him to look up at her.

"What's so funny?" he asked.

"Old enough to be my father, huh? So that would make you, what? Fifty-one? Fifty-two?"

"Lord, no."

"Well, then I think it's safe to say you're not even close. I'm guessin' you're closer to forty than you are to fifty."

"That right?" he asked, liking the way she was still regarding him with that look. The one that said she wouldn't mind if he stripped her naked right there in the kitchen and tossed her on the table.

He was considering it himself.

"Do you have an issue with age?" Kenzie asked.

Damn right, he did. He'd been burned by a woman who had been fifteen years younger than him, one he'd had no business being with in the first place, but sometimes the heart wanted what the heart wanted.

"Ah. So it's like that," Kenzie said, obviously tired of waiting for him to answer. "I'm twenty-six, Lucas. Not that it matters one damn bit."

Lucas could tell by her tone that he'd upset her. "I was in junior high school when you were born."

"Fantastic," she said sarcastically. "Well, since we're clearly declaring our location for specific events, then I'll go next. I was kissing you a few minutes ago in my bedroom."

Lucas laughed. He couldn't help himself. The woman's wit amused him. "You win."

"Yep, I do. Kissing trumps junior high school any day."

They were both silent for a moment, and Lucas knew he needed to go. He needed to put a little distance between himself and this little wildcat. It'd been a long damn time since he'd met a woman he wanted to wrangle. But with Kenzie, he wasn't sure that either of them would survive that sort of relationship intact.

Lord have mercy. Now he was thinking about relationships.

Fuck, he was old. And delusional.

Pushing to his feet, Lucas smiled down at her. Her smile fell, and he instantly regretted his decision to go, but he knew it was for the best. "I need to get back to the house," he told her.

Kenzie nodded her head, but she didn't move to get up. "Maybe I'll see you around."

Hopefully. Lucas didn't tell her that, though. "It's possible. Keep that knee clean, and stay off the ice. Won't heal if you keep splittin' it open."

"Yes, doctor."

Lucas laughed again before grabbing his coat and heading toward the front door. He needed to go before he did something incredibly stupid. Like take her back to that bedroom.

"Does Ralph still handle things around here?" he asked when she fell into step behind him.

"Yeah. Without him, I'm pretty sure the cows would be dead at this point and the chickens would be running free in town. I'm not good with those, I promise you that much."

Lucas shrugged into his coat as he made his way through the small, cheery living room. He didn't respond to her statement, again at a loss for words.

"Oh, and Lucas," Kenzie called from behind him.

With his hand on the doorknob, he slowly glanced over his shoulder.

"I don't usually do this," she told him, her hand circling as though she were referencing the room, her expression serious.

"Do what?" he questioned.

"Blind dates. One-night stands. Inviting strange men to my bedroom. Take your pick. I've never done any of those things before."

Holy hell. Lucas's heart missed a beat at the significance of what she was telling him. She'd never had a one-night stand, yet a short while ago, they'd been in her bedroom, damn close to making it to the bed.

He wanted to ask her why she'd chosen him, but he decided against it. He didn't want to know the answer. Didn't need another reason to want to stay.

So, he merely nodded his head in understanding before pulling the front door open.

Son of a bitch.

The sleet was coming down heavily, his truck covered in a thick layer of ice already. He glanced down at the driveway to see it was also covered.

Kenzie moved up beside him, ducking beneath his arm to peer outside. "Looks like you won't be goin' anywhere for a while. Gettin' out of the driveway when it's dry is hard enough."

Shit.

As much as he wanted to argue, to just walk out to his truck and drive back to his house, he knew she was right. If he tried, he'd end up in a ditch somewhere, just like she had earlier. Or maybe that was just an excuse.

Kenzie took a step back, leaving him standing at the open door. He hesitated for another second, maybe two, but then he closed it and turned back to face her.

It was time to be honest.

Because otherwise, he feared that one of them was going to get hurt.

Or worse ... both of them.

Chapter Seven

Kenzie wasn't sure if it was her lucky day or if the universe was just playing a cruel trick on her. But the fact that Lucas was now stranded at her place was both intriguing and frightening. Not because she was scared of him. Quite the opposite, in fact. She wanted him with a passion she wasn't sure she had ever felt before. Definitely not in a long time, for sure.

But he did not look at all happy about being stuck there with her, and that bothered her more than she was willing to admit.

"Don't worry," she said softly. "I promise not to jump you when you least expect it."

A sexy smile curled the edges of Lucas's beautiful mouth, and she couldn't help but answer with a smile of her own.

"Trust me, darlin', that's the least of my worries."

"Then what's got you lookin' like you're ready to fight the elements just to get away from me?" she asked honestly.

Lucas studied her for a moment, not saying anything. Kenzie figured he wasn't going to answer, but he finally opened his mouth. But he closed it just as quickly.

"It's all right," she told him. "No need to answer that. I'm sure you don't want to hurt my feelings."

Kenzie started toward the kitchen but was pulled up short when Lucas spoke.

"Darlin', the last thing I'm worried about is your feelings." She was facing away from him, but she heard his boots on the hardwood as he moved closer. She held her breath, waiting to see what he'd say next.

He didn't disappoint.

Lucas's big, warm hands gripped her shoulders gently as he urged her to face him. She allowed him to maneuver her easily, turning to look up at him.

"I don't wanna hurt you," Lucas whispered, his voice rough with emotion, which surprised her. "I'd give my right arm to take you back there and make love to you for the rest of the day, Kenzie. That's not the issue."

"Then what is?" she asked, forcing the words past her dry throat.

"Tomorrow," he answered simply.

Kenzie nodded, understanding. He wasn't going to make her any promises, but she knew, even though she knew little about this man, she knew that wasn't how he was made. Someone had hurt him, and he didn't trust easily.

And she wasn't one to make promises, either. Not when it came to relationships. She hadn't been looking for one when he'd just happened to drop into her world, and she'd be lying if she said she wasn't interested. But she didn't want to get hurt, either.

Committing to a one-night stand with this man would be the worst thing she could do, because tomorrow, when he slipped out her door, she would want him to come back. She would want to see him, to be with him ... and clearly, based on what he was telling her, that wasn't an option.

"More coffee?" she asked, trying to break the uncomfortable tension that cloaked them like a scratchy wool blanket.

Lucas studied her face, his eyes trailing down to her lips, and she felt that inferno encompass them both. Despite their fears, this was going to happen. She knew it and he knew it.

The question was ... were they going to give in easily? Or were they going to put up a fight?

Lucas answered the question for her when he slid his knuckles across her cheek and then cupped the back of her head, pulling her to him. Kenzie gave in, unable to resist him.

The kiss started slow. Sweet and gentle. But then, within seconds, it intensified tenfold.

"Kenzie," Lucas whispered against her lips. "Tell me we shouldn't do this."

Kenzie heard the emotion in his tone, and it called to her. This might be the biggest mistake they ever made, but she couldn't resist him. She didn't want to send him away. But she couldn't lie to him, either. "We shouldn't do this." Pressing her lips to his once again, she wrapped her arms around his neck, her breasts pressing against the hard planes of his chest.

When he pulled back a few moments later, they were both trying to suck in air. Their eyes met, locked, and Kenzie knew that the decision had been made for them both. Taking a step back, Lucas's hand slid down to his side, but Kenzie didn't hesitate. She reached for him, linking her fingers with his and leading him toward her bedroom.

Again.

There was no denying the attraction was there, the chemistry off the charts. They were both right where they wanted to be. And it was high time she took the reins, made the decision that she would normally avoid because she didn't want to get hurt.

"Are you sure about this, darlin'?" Lucas asked when they stepped into her bedroom for the second time that day.

Rather than answer, Kenzie reached for the hem of her shirt and lifted, pulling it over her head and tossing it to the floor.

His jacket was the next article of clothing to be discarded, but as he removed it, Lucas never took his eyes off her.

Kenzie reached around behind her and unhooked her bra, allowing it to slide down her arms and drop to the floor beside her shirt.

Then, as though it was one for one, Lucas made the next move, toeing off his boots, his eyes glued to her bare chest. Warmth pooled in her bloodstream as the temperature in the room soared from the pure passion she witnessed in his penetrating gaze.

Kenzie reached for the button on her shorts, slowly working it free before lowering the zipper and then allowing the denim to drop to the floor.

Lucas reached behind his head, grabbed a handful of his shirt, and pulled the dark gray cotton over his head, dropping it to the floor.

Kenzie's mouth dropped open as she stared at his naked upper body. She'd never seen a man built quite like him. At least not in person. His pecs were two hard planes, his abs perfectly bisected and cut, his biceps bulging. In a single word, he was perfection, a man whose body was honed from hard work, and she found she was reduced to nothing more than a jumble of out-of-control hormones.

Kenzie slipped her fingers beneath the band of her panties, pushing them down and then allowing them to drop to the floor with the rest of her clothing. She was then standing in front of him completely naked, the heat from his gaze warming her although the room was cold.

Lucas pulled his wallet from his back pocket, tossing it onto the bed before shedding his jeans and underwear at the same time, taking his socks off in the process. And then he was just as naked as she was.

Unable to look away, Kenzie remained rooted to the floor, her eyes raking over every delicious inch of him starting at his sexy feet and ending on his beautiful eyes. He continued to look at her, and Kenzie wasn't sure what to do or say, but she wanted him to touch her, wanted to feel the rough scrape of his hands against her skin. The tension fizzled inside her, making her hands shake and her breaths become labored.

The next thing she knew, Lucas was moving closer, his hands cupping her face again as he turned her head up to face him. "You're the most beautiful woman I've ever seen," he whispered.

His words were so matter-of-fact she had no choice but to believe him. Rather than say anything in response, Kenzie pushed up on her toes, meeting his lips. She slid her arms around his trim waist, her hands stroking up his back and then back down, the feel of hard muscles flexing beneath her palms. She had expected the passion to consume them instantly, but somehow — clearly he had more willpower than she did — Lucas managed to keep the kiss slow and gentle, the hunger surging just beneath the surface.

He backed her toward the bed, and when her knees hit the mattress, she kept herself upright. Barely. Holding on to him, she thrust her tongue against his, devouring him as the electrical current that arched between their bodies grew stronger, more potent. Seconds passed, and then Kenzie found herself on her back on the bed, Lucas's huge, hard body looming above her.

She felt the steely length of him pressing against her belly, but he wasn't trying to rush things. He seemed content to kiss her, his hands still not venturing anywhere.

"Touch me, Lucas," she pleaded when he pulled back, their eyes meeting in the dim light.

"My pleasure," he said gruffly, his mouth sliding down her jaw, her neck. He pressed light kisses against her collarbone, then drifted lower to the tops of her breasts.

Kenzie bowed her back, trying to get his mouth where she wanted it. His sexy chuckle made her pussy spasm with need. And when his lips wrapped around one distended nipple, Kenzie cried out, the sensation overwhelming her.

"Oh, God, that feels... Lucas, don't stop," she begged, gripping his head and pulling him to her chest, forcing her nipple into his mouth. He teased the tip with his tongue, and her body heated even more than she thought possible.

When he released her nipple from his mouth, she groaned.

"Don't worry, darlin', I'm just gettin' started."

Lucas proved himself when his mouth ventured to her other breast, sucking it into his mouth and then nipping her with his teeth, sending a bolt of pleasure-pain ricocheting straight to her clit.

Oh, yeah, she was a goner.

Chapter Eight

Lucas was doing his damnedest not to devour Kenzie whole. From the moment she'd started pulling off her clothes, he'd been at a loss for words. And breath. She'd stolen the air directly from his lungs as she'd stripped in front of him. She was, by far, the most beautiful woman he'd ever had the pleasure of laying his eyes on.

And now, with her sweet body writhing beneath his, he was hard-pressed to keep from taking her hard, trying not to rush things, desperate to savor her with his mouth and his hands before he lost complete control. He wanted to take his time, to taste every delicious inch of her creamy skin, but her soft moans were making his dick throb with a devastating need.

His head was whirling with a million thoughts, yet he was doing his best to stay right there in the moment.

Sliding his mouth down Kenzie's flat, smooth belly, he continued on his path, wanting to give her everything, to take everything she had to give, but he was holding part of himself back. He couldn't help it. As much as he wanted her, as desperate as he was to bury himself in her slick warmth, his heart was telling him to stop, to retreat before he found himself in a situation he wouldn't be able to walk away from.

It was true, Lucas loved hard when he loved, and although he hardly knew this woman, he feared she was going to be the next one to take a piece of him that he'd never be able to get back.

"Lucas."

Kenzie's voice pulled him from his thoughts, and that was when he realized he was kneeling between her thighs, staring down at her.

"Come here," she instructed, holding her arms out to him.

He moved toward her, lowering himself over her once again, and when her fingers wrapped around his erection, he hissed out a breath.

"Please tell me you have a condom," Kenzie said, her voice soft, her eyes locked with his.

He nodded, but honestly, he could hardly make out what she was saying. The way she stroked him, it was almost more than he could handle. Aside from his own hand, he hadn't had anyone touch him like that in … months.

"Quit thinking so much," Kenzie whispered.

Lucas tried to shake off the thoughts, opting to slide his hands over the comforter, trying to locate his wallet. He knew he'd tossed it there earlier.

Kenzie lifted her hand, holding it out to him, and he looked at her, drowning in the sweet expression on her face.

Yeah, there was no doubt about it, he was about to have his heart torn to shreds, and the worst part about it, he wasn't able to do a damn thing to stop it, because, more than he'd wanted anything in so damn long, Lucas wanted Kenzie.

Every part of her.

Retrieving the condom from his wallet, Lucas made quick work of opening it and then rolling it on, taking his position above Kenzie once again. This time, when she reached between them and found his cock, he sucked in a breath. And when she guided him to her entrance, his head started spinning.

"Make love to me, Lucas," she said in the softest, sweetest voice he'd ever heard.

As he slid into her slowly, one inch at a time, Lucas's entire body went rigid. She was so hot, so tight, so wet... He wasn't sure he was going to last long enough to make this good for her.

But he was certainly going to try.

Kenzie's arms wound around his neck, pulling him down to her until their mouths met. When her tongue slipped into his mouth, he pressed his hips against hers, burying himself to the hilt. When she moaned into his mouth, he once again fought the urge to retreat and then slam into her.

Barely.

Kenzie began rocking her hips beneath him, her mouth fused to his, her arms wreathing his neck, her fingers tangling in his hair, and Lucas lost every ounce of control he possessed. Pushing up onto his arms so he could look at her, he withdrew and then drove into her. Not as hard as he wanted to, but hard enough to pull a gasp from her.

"Yes," she moaned. "You feel so good."

Lucas didn't say a word, relishing the warm grip of her pussy. He continued to fuck her, slowly at first, but his pace quickly increased as the pleasure overwhelmed him. Her body gripped him tightly, pulling him deeper. The look in her beautiful eyes as she watched him had something akin to hope filling his chest.

This was more than sex.

He'd never been one to believe in love at first sight, although he hadn't been able to explain the myriad of thoughts he'd had about this woman since the night he'd met her. And now, right here in her bedroom, while he made love to her, he had to wonder whether or not there was a thread of truth to that saying. Because as much as he wanted to deny it, he was falling for her.

And he didn't even give a shit that he knew very little about her.

As far as he was concerned, he knew enough.

Kenzie surprised him with her strength when she managed to flip their positions, placing him on his back while she knelt above him, his dick still lodged deep inside her. It was his turn to groan when she began to rock forward and back, driving him deeper.

"Lucas." The way she said his name, almost reverently, had him pulling himself fully to the moment. Sliding his hands up to rest on her thighs, he guided her right where he needed her to be, watching the way her breasts swayed above him, the way her eyes continued to rake over his face. She never looked away, and that left him with another feeling … one that he couldn't very well name.

"Oh, God, Lucas. I'm gonna…"

He didn't need her to finish the sentence, because her body told him everything he needed to know. Her pussy clamped down on him. Hard. Milking his release from him as he thrust up into her once, twice... On the third time he drove his hips upward, his own climax took him, leaving his mind blank.

Twenty minutes later, Lucas was lying in Kenzie's bed, holding her in his arms. After he had disposed of the condom and taken a few minutes to wash up, he had returned to the bedroom to find her still there, still watching him.

"Don't leave," she had told him.

"I don't plan to." Where the words came from, he didn't know, but as soon as they were out there, he realized they were true. And it had nothing to do with the fact he'd be battling the elements if he opted to leave.

He didn't want to go.

Not yet, anyway.

After crawling back into bed with her, Lucas tried to give himself over to sleep, but it never came. Not even two hours later when Kenzie was still passed out in his arms. Trying not to wake her, he managed to untangle himself from her and grab his clothes from the floor before slipping out of her room and into the living room. It was late afternoon, but the gray clouds had darkened the sky more than it had been that morning. Because they'd spent the better part of the afternoon hidden away in her bedroom, he had no idea how the roads were, but he was seriously contemplating chancing it and leaving.

As shitty as that was.

After pulling on his jeans and his shirt, Lucas planted his ass on the couch in Kenzie's living room to pull on his boots. Kenzie's cat made its way over to him, winding around his feet and meowing up at him.

"What?" he asked the cat.

"Meow."

"Well, that ain't all that helpful," he replied to the fat gray cat, tugging on one boot and lowering his pant leg over it.

"Meow."

"Unless you're gonna tell me not to go, I'm not lookin' for your input," he said softly, pulling on his other boot.

"Don't go."

Lucas looked up to see Kenzie standing in the doorway that led to the hall. She was wrapped in a blanket, her blonde hair mussed, her rich brown eyes slumberous.

He didn't know what to say to her, but he couldn't look away.

"If Jasper won't ask, I will," she said softly, moving toward him.

Lucas planted his elbows on his knees and dropped his head into his hands. He was so damn confused. Mostly because what had transpired between them from the moment he'd picked her up on the side of the road had caught him completely off guard.

But he wasn't interested in a relationship, not even something based on intense sexual chemistry, and he knew that, if nothing else, he and Kenzie had that.

She lowered herself to the couch beside him, her hand sliding onto his thigh. It wasn't a sexual touch, more soothing than anything. Her scent flooded his senses, and he sighed. "Kenzie, I just don't know how to do this."

"To do what?" she asked, her confusion echoing in her tone.

"I don't know how to give you what you want."

Kenzie chuckled. "What *I* want?"

He offered her a sideways glance, fearful of what he would see on her face.

"I don't recall announcing what I want from you," Kenzie said simply when their eyes met. "So don't try and push this off on me."

Lucas realized that was exactly what he was doing. He was projecting his own fears and making this into something that it wasn't. What the hell was he so worried about? It wasn't like he'd fallen in love with this woman. Not in one night.

No fucking way.

Shit.

Lucas got to his feet, pacing the floor while Kenzie and her cat sat on her couch and watched him, their eyes moving back and forth, back and forth with every sweep he made of the room.

"What is it that you're runnin' from?" Kenzie asked after a minute or two.

Lucas stopped and stared at her. "Nothin'," he lied, the word leaving a bad taste in his mouth.

"Liar."

Stopping mid-stride, Lucas just stared at the stunning woman with her disheveled hair, her naked shoulders visible above the sheet that was falling ever so slightly down her arms.

God, where had she come from? Had she been sent there just to torture him? She seemed to do the exact opposite of everything he expected her to do. She didn't coddle him, didn't beg him to stay. And she called him on his lies. She was the opposite of…

Fucking hell.

That was what his problem was. He was still living in the past, still harboring hatred for a woman who'd done him wrong. But Kenzie wasn't Brenda. She wasn't anything like her, and he had no idea how he could peg her so accurately after knowing her for only a short period of time, but it was true. He knew it was. She was straightforward and honest, and he was…

An idiot.

So why was he making it harder than it needed to be? At thirty-eight years old, Lucas was too damn old to play games with women, yet he was the one who'd instigated this one.

Chapter Nine

Kenzie felt almost as though she were watching a wounded animal after it'd been cornered and had no idea which way to go to get free. From the moment she'd woken up to find Lucas had slipped out of bed, she had known he was back to that place in his head. The same place he'd been when he'd taken her to her bedroom the first time.

Clearly the guy didn't do things like this, which Kenzie could easily relate to; however, she had never been on this side of the relationship. She would never claim to be perfect, but usually the men she dated were the ones who latched on at the beginning and didn't seem to let go no matter how hard she tried to loosen their grip. Why that was, she had no idea.

Lucas, on the other hand, looked sincerely perplexed on how to handle what was happening between them. And there was definitely something happening between them.

"When was the last time you were in a relationship?" Kenzie asked, the question slipping right out of her mouth before she had a chance to reel it back into her brain.

"It's been a while," Lucas admitted, still sounding defeated.

"How long's 'a while'?"

"Nine months," he informed her.

"Your definition of 'a while' and mine certainly are a little different," Kenzie said, trying to lighten the mood. "She did a number on you, huh?"

Lucas's glistening green eyes zoomed in on her, and Kenzie fought the urge to squirm. He seemed both intense and a little lost as he penetrated her with his stern gaze. There was certainly a vulnerability to Lucas, which Kenzie found oddly sexy.

To her surprise, he answered her. "Yeah, she did."

"How long were y'all together?"

"Thirteen years."

Wow. Okay. So, she certainly hadn't been anticipating that.

Kenzie couldn't keep her jaw from damn near hitting the floor. "Do you … uh… Do you have kids?" She didn't know where the question came from, but as soon as she said it, she dreaded his answer.

"No kids."

The relief that swept through her was overwhelming. It wasn't that she would mind him having children of his own. She'd never been the kind of woman who wouldn't be with a single father, but for some reason, the idea of Lucas not having children with another woman soothed something oddly possessive within her.

"Married?" Kenzie questioned.

"Divorced," Lucas responded instantly. "She left me for another man."

Kenzie nodded, understanding. It sucked, truly. "Her loss," she said automatically.

Obviously that caught Lucas by surprise, because his eyes widened.

"What is this? This thing we've started," he asked.

"No idea," she admitted truthfully. If she knew what this was, she wouldn't be as confused as he was. "Does it have to be anything?"

"For me, it does," Lucas replied, and this time, it was Kenzie's turn to be surprised.

Not only was Lucas Burch handsome, sexy, and amazing in bed, he was also … honest. Which was refreshing.

"For me, too," she told him softly.

"What do we do now?"

"Dinner?" she asked, a small smile forming on her lips.

Lucas laughed, just as she'd hoped he would.

"I've never met another woman like you, Kenzie."

The truth in Lucas's gaze had Kenzie rooted in place, clutching the blanket tightly to her chest. Her heart was beating twice as fast and three times as hard as normal. She felt as though she'd just finished working out, but the most she'd done was hold the blanket against her naked body, hoping she was covered. But still, he made her feel completely naked, entirely vulnerable.

"I want to take that as a compliment," she told him.

"You should."

"Does that mean you'll let me cook you dinner?"

"Only if I can help."

"A man who knows his way around the kitchen." Kenzie smiled brightly. "I've never met another man like you, Lucas."

His laugh reverberated through the living room, making every muscle in Kenzie's body loosen in relief. She had no idea what it was about this man or why she didn't want him to leave, but it was true. He could stay there forever as far as she was concerned. It was a shocking revelation, because in all of her adult life, never had she felt anything like this for a man. Probably nothing even remotely close.

Lucas pulled off his coat and tossed it to the couch when Kenzie stood.

"Just give me a second to get dressed."

Lucas shocked her when he pulled his shirt over his head and reached for the button on his jeans. They were standing not two feet apart, right there in the living room, and he was undressing. When he toed off his boots and pulled another condom out of his wallet, she knew that getting dressed was going to have to wait.

Giving in to her need for him, Kenzie moved closer, keeping the blanket firmly around her. When Lucas was naked and he had sheathed himself with the condom, he took a step closer, sliding his hands beneath the blanket and planting them firmly on her hips.

"I'm not sure I'll ever get enough of you," Lucas said quietly, the rough scrape of his five-o'clock shadow against her cheek sending electrical sparks through her nerve endings. The way his calloused hands caressed her hips so reverently made Kenzie want to burrow into him and never let him go.

"Ditto," she replied, unlatching her arms and wrapping them around him, keeping the blanket around herself.

Lucas turned and then lowered himself to the couch, pulling her closer as he did. When she was straddling his hips, a shudder ran through her. When he guided himself inside her, Kenzie's body tightened, the exquisite pleasure causing a tremor to start at her core.

"Ahh, damn, Kenzie," he said gruffly. "Baby, you feel so good."

She decided she liked this vocal side of Lucas. As she'd learned, he wasn't a man of many words. Earlier, when they'd made love, he'd hardly said anything, but now, with every gruff rasp of his voice, Kenzie's body was burning brighter, hotter.

"Ride me, Kenzie."

Oh, Lord, the man was going to make her go off like a bottle rocket if he kept talking like that. She began rocking her hips, taking him deeper into her body. She released the blanket, allowing it to fall to the floor. Planting her hands on his broad shoulders, Kenzie controlled the pace, keeping her eyes locked with his while she indulged in all his body could offer her.

"That's it, baby. Fuck, that feels good."

Kenzie couldn't speak. Her breath was lodged in her throat; the pleasure was nearly more than she could bear. And when Lucas began thrusting his hips upward, driving himself impossibly deep inside her, Kenzie's body began to tremble, her orgasm building until it took over.

"Lucas!" She barely managed to get his name past her lips when her climax tore through her, sending her soaring.

"You're so beautiful when you come, Kenzie. So damn beautiful." His voice was laced with gravel and so damn sexy. Kenzie clung to every word, letting it take her even higher than before.

"I'm gonna come, Kenzie. Oh, God, baby." Lucas's voice cracked on the last couple of words, his fingers digging into the flesh of her hips as he stilled, his hips jerking.

Kenzie's inner muscles clamped down on him, and another orgasm broke loose just as he came inside her.

While she tried to catch her breath, Kenzie realized two things. One, she had no idea what this was between them, and two, she prayed he stuck around long enough for them both to find out.

Chapter Ten

ddly, dinner with Kenzie was far more comfortable than Lucas had anticipated. Not that he had expected Kenzie to do anything to put him on edge, but more because he'd expected the worst. Nothing new, though. He'd been waiting for the other shoe to drop since the second he'd stepped foot in her house earlier in the day.

He wasn't used to this sort of interaction with a woman. After his marriage to Brenda had dissolved, Lucas had gone on a bender, falling into bed with several women over the course of just two months. Nothing more than one night, and certainly none of those encounters had involved dinner. But with Kenzie, even if the roads had been clear enough for him to leave — and truth was, with his four-wheel-drive truck, he could've navigated his way out of there if he had really wanted to — Lucas found he didn't want to leave.

Even when he'd been at war with himself, having an inane conversation with a cat, he hadn't wanted to walk out Kenzie's front door for fear he wouldn't be welcome back.

And now that they'd finished dinner and night had settled in, Kenzie had put on another pot of coffee. She'd insisted that he head to the living room after he had helped her do the dishes, so that was where he was, sitting on the couch, looking around the room, taking it all in. He liked the simplicity of Kenzie's house. There was minimal decor, but there were pictures on nearly every surface. Almost all of them had Kenzie's beautiful, smiling face in them.

Much different than his own place, which was pretty empty after Brenda had taken damn near everything they'd acquired over the years. Not that he'd tried to stop her. The only thing he gave a shit about was the ranch. It had been in his family for generations, and he damn sure wasn't going to let her steal it out from underneath him. So, by the time all was said and done, he'd kept the ranch and his truck. The rest of the shit, he'd let her take, with the agreement that he would never have to see her again.

"What're you thinkin' about?"

Lucas looked up to see Kenzie approaching. She was wearing the pink cotton robe she'd donned after their last encounter on the couch and carrying two coffee mugs. Reaching out, he took them both from her and set them on the coffee table before pulling her down beside him. Wrapping his arm around her, he let her get comfortable. She was sitting sideways, her back against his side, her knees drawn up, her cute feet propped on the couch. She reached for the mugs, handing him one first and then taking the other.

"Just thinkin'," he told her.

"I got that part. What about?"

"My ex-wife."

Lucas felt Kenzie's body tense slightly, and he patted her knee. "Not like that. I guess I just realized how much shit I'd been hangin' on to all these months."

"Y'all were together a long time. It seems natural for you to still be hung up on her."

"It ain't like that," he assured her. "When I found out she'd been cheatin', I was more than willing to show her the door."

"I'm sorry," Kenzie said softly.

"Don't be. If she hadn't cheated…" Lucas caught his next words before they could slip out of his mouth.

"What?" Kenzie asked, twisting around so she could look at him.

He sighed. Why the hell did he have to get involved so damn quickly? Why couldn't he just let this be fun and games? It seemed that, although she insisted she'd never done this before and he believed her, Kenzie was more than willing to take things slow. And maybe that was the issue. He didn't want casual.

"If she hadn't cheated, I wouldn't be here now."

"No, I guess you wouldn't. Well, if that's the way we're thinkin' about it, then I'm glad she cheated. God, that sounded crass. Sorry again," Kenzie stated, chuckling.

When she yawned, Lucas knew it was time for bed. "You're tired," he said. "I guess I should really be going." Not that he wanted to, but it seemed the appropriate thing to say. He didn't want to invite himself to stay.

Fortunately, he didn't have to, because Kenzie solved his dilemma by insisting that he stay. She didn't use the weather as an excuse, and neither did he. When she got up from the couch, Lucas took her hand and allowed her to lead him to her bedroom once again. As much as he wanted to make love to her again, his body was tired, his mind even more so. She must've known, because Kenzie simply stripped out of her robe, her naked body revealed before she climbed into bed, pulling the covers up over her while she waited for him to join her.

Which he did. Without a second of hesitation.

When the gray light of morning slipped in through the windows in Kenzie's bedroom, Lucas forced his eyes open. The warm woman sprawled over him was an instant reminder of where he was. The immediate swelling in his chest told him why he was still there. Not to mention the swelling that was happening in other regions. It was difficult not to react to Kenzie's nearness. The woman did something to him, and like he'd told her yesterday, he wasn't sure that he'd ever get enough of her.

Ever.

"Mornin'," Kenzie greeted him in a sleepy, soft tone, making him smile. She pushed her hair out of her face and looked up at him. "I sure hope you slept at least a little."

"All night," he told her. In fact, he couldn't remember the last time he'd slept quite so deeply.

"Good," she said, a small smile curling the corners of her pretty pink lips.

"Why good?" he asked, noting the mischievous gleam in her chocolate-brown eyes.

"I want to make sure you're good and rested."

"For?"

"First a shower, then … you know."

Lucas pressed his face into the crook of her neck, inhaling her sweet scent. "No, I don't know. Why don't you enlighten me?"

Without words, Kenzie told him her intentions when she slid her hand down his stomach, her smooth, cool fingers wrapping around his dick and stroking him lightly. He groaned, his hips thrusting toward her touch, encouraging her to continue.

"Does that feel good?" she asked, turning her head and giving him better access to her neck.

"So fucking good," he admitted. "Don't stop."

"I don't plan to, cowboy."

Kenzie continued to tease him ruthlessly, never applying enough friction to bring him to the edge, but continuing to drive him crazy with her soft, gentle touch.

"Why don't we kill two birds with one stone?" he asked when he knew he needed more of her.

"How do you plan to do that?" she asked.

"Let's shower together."

Kenzie turned to look at him, her eyes meeting his, her smile radiant. "I like the way you think."

Within seconds, he was following her to the bathroom. He snatched the last condom he had in his wallet as he followed her. Once the water heated, he joined her in the oversized shower and then attempted to reacquaint himself with her body by using his hands. And his mouth.

Backing her against the tiled wall, Lucas lifted her leg and planted her foot on the small ledge before he dropped to his knees and buried his face between her thighs.

"Lucas. That feels… Oh, God, that feels so good. Too good."

Kenzie's soft moans grew louder as he teased her clit with his tongue, working her up but never giving her enough to send her over. He would, but only after he got his fill. Slipping two fingers inside her, Lucas continued to flick her clit with his tongue while fucking her slowly until she was thrusting her hips forward.

"Lucas! I'm gonna come!"

And she did, her entire body tightening, her pussy clamping down on his fingers, but Lucas didn't relent, continuing to lick and suck her clit until she forced his head away, twining her fingers into his hair and pulling him upward.

With a chuckle, he got to his feet, crushing his body to hers, melding his lips to hers.

"Condom," she whispered against his mouth.

"One step ahead of you, darlin'." Lucas managed to slide the condom on and, within seconds, was plowing into her, holding her knee against his hip, opening her up so he could drive deep. With her arms wrapped around his neck, her mouth sealed to his, he inhaled her while at the same time tried to bury himself as deep as physically possible. It didn't take long before she was crying out his name again, and the beautiful sound sent him right over the edge.

Twenty minutes later, after getting dressed, Lucas joined Kenzie in the kitchen. She had already pulled out bacon and eggs and was preparing them near the sink while a skillet sat on the stainless steel stovetop, the gas flame beneath it flickering.

"Good morning," she greeted, shooting him a smile over her shoulder.

Something loosened in Lucas's chest as he looked at her. He really liked this woman. He liked her wit, her easy banter, the way she kept a positive outlook, even when the chips were stacked against her, like when her car had gone into the ditch. He liked the graceful way she moved, the sweet smile that she was quick to offer him.

Hell, Lucas figured it was safe to say that he liked everything he knew about her so far. But there were still some questions he had for her. Some answers he knew could change everything that was building between them.

"So how do you like it here in Embers Ridge?" he asked straightforwardly as he grabbed two glasses from the cabinet and poured orange juice from a pitcher in the refrigerator.

Kenzie didn't answer immediately. She continued cracking eggs and whipping them with a fork, her attention divided between him and the stove. With his glass in hand, he leaned against the counter not far from where she was working and watched her, waiting for her answer.

"Until yesterday, I have to admit, I hadn't felt as though I fit in all that well."

Well, that was honest. He liked honest. Lucas didn't say anything, because she continued.

"I don't get out much, and the only person who visits is my mother."

"Do you talk to Ralph much?" Lucas asked.

"Sometimes. But honestly, that old cowboy talks less than you do," she told him as she poured the eggs into the skillet and then laid bacon across a griddle on another burner.

Lucas grinned. Yeah, he could see that.

"But aside from the lack of companionship, I do like it here. It's a much slower pace than what I was used to in Houston."

Lucas realized then that he had no idea what it was Kenzie did for a living. How she could easily uproot herself from Houston to move to a small town. "What about work? Do you miss it?"

"No," Kenzie said with a smile. "But that's because I took it with me. I'm a medical transcriptionist."

"How the hell do you do that?" Lucas found himself asking before he could think better of it.

"Well … you transcribe the—"

Lucas cut her off, leaning over and giving her a quick kiss, mainly because he couldn't resist the urge to do so, before stepping back out of her way. "I know how it's done. I'm tryin' to understand why."

"Someone's gotta do it," Kenzie said, her gaze meeting his. "More importantly, I get to work from home. So like I said, if it weren't for the lack of a social life, it wouldn't be much different than my life back in Houston."

Neither of them said anything for a few minutes. Lucas continued to watch her while she worked, and while she focused on scrambling the eggs, he flipped the bacon and then pulled each slice off when it was done. A few minutes later, they were sitting at her kitchen table, her cat meowing from the floor.

"You've got food," Kenzie told the cat, and as though the animal had needed her to explain that, she padded off to the other side of the kitchen, leaving them to eat in peace.

When they were both nearly finished with the food, Lucas went back to their earlier conversation.

"Have you considered goin' back to Houston?" That was the question he truly wanted an answer to. As quickly as he found himself interested in this woman, the idea of her leaving to go back to Houston caused his stomach to churn.

"As of now, no," Kenzie replied. "I'm gonna stick it out. I like the small town, the people I've met, the solitude I'm afforded out here. So, no, I haven't considered going back."

"Good to know."

"Is it?" Kenzie asked, her eyes searching his.

"Yes," he told her honestly. "I still don't know what to make of this, but I'm too damned old to waste a whole helluva lot of time on casual relationships, Kenzie." He wasn't sure honesty was the best way to go at this point, but he truly didn't know any other way to do it. After Brenda had knocked his world off its axis with her unfaithfulness, Lucas hadn't been sure he'd ever want to settle down again. But the fact of the matter was, he was a one-woman man. Always had been.

"Well, if you want my opinion—"

Kenzie's statement was cut off by a pounding at the front of the house. She quickly jumped to her feet, securing her robe around herself and making her way to the door. She tossed him a look that reflected her confusion. Clearly she had no idea who would be knocking on her door this early in the morning.

Lucas got to his feet, thankful he'd gotten dressed before they'd had breakfast. When he heard a man's voice from the other side of the door, something dark and possessive took root in his soul, and he found himself moving closer to Kenzie.

When he approached, she took a step back and opened the door.

"Oh, Mr. Burch. I'm so glad you're here. I saw your truck."

Lucas recognized Ralph instantly. "Is there a problem?"

"Yes, sir," Ralph said, his raspy tone reflecting the fact that he was a lifelong smoker. "One of the horses is stuck in the creek. Can't get her out."

Lucas glanced at Kenzie. He noticed she looked as though someone had told her that her cat had died.

"Let me get my boots," he told Ralph, spinning around and heading to the couch, where he'd left his boots the night before.

Kenzie invited Ralph inside, closing the door behind him, and then she disappeared down the hall to her bedroom. He was shocked to see her coming back toward him as he was shrugging into his coat and planting his Stetson on his head.

"I'm gonna help," she informed him.

He wasn't sure what to say to that. He hadn't expected her to volunteer. Had she been his ex-wife, she would've been chastising him for having to go out in the weather, more because she wanted him to cater to her hand and foot than because he actually was going to deal with the elements in order to take care of an animal.

"Get your coat on," Lucas instructed her. "You got a hat?"

Kenzie didn't answer. Instead, she turned on her heels and hurried back down the hall. When she returned, she had a black hoodie on, the hood pulled up over her head, and she was sliding her arms into a heavy jacket. He was happy to see she wasn't wearing shorts as she had been yesterday.

Damn, had that been just yesterday? Holy hell. It seemed like a lifetime had passed since he'd run into her at the pharmacy.

When Ralph cleared his throat, Lucas remembered what he was supposed to be doing. Taking her hand, he led her out the front door, following Ralph, who was already making a beeline for his truck, moving as fast as his seventy-year-old bones could carry him. Lucas wasn't all that surprised to see the man still had a spring in his step.

Part of him wondered if he'd be able to keep up with the old man. The thought made him smile.

Chapter Eleven

Kenzie hung on for dear life as Ralph steered his truck across the bumpy ground, making his way behind the guesthouse, where he had lived for more years than Kenzie could remember, toward the creek that ran through the back half of her grandparents' land. She was sandwiched between Ralph and Lucas on the single bench seat of the old, rusted Ford, doing her best not to flop onto either man while she gripped the dashboard with both hands.

She had no idea what she could possibly do to help either of these men once they finally got to their destination, but she knew without a doubt that she couldn't just sit at her house and wait for them to come back. This was her property, her cows, her horses, her chickens. She was responsible for them, and though she didn't know much about how to care for them yet, she'd made it her mission to learn everything there was to learn. She regretted not spending enough time with her grandfather, learning the lay of the land prior to his passing, and she felt she owed it to him to give everything she had to continuing his legacy.

"Oh, my God," Kenzie said on a long exhale when the horse came into view. One of the fences was knocked down, and sure enough, the horse had wandered down into the creek and was now stuck, the rushing water up to the underside of its belly.

She had fully expected both men to tell her to stay put, but they didn't, and she wasn't sure what to make of that. But she didn't have time to think about it, because when the truck came to a jerky stop, Lucas jumped out, and she was right behind him. It was obvious he knew what he was doing, so she didn't bother to question him, just hoped he would tell her what to do when and if he needed her help. The rain was coming down heavily, but it wasn't frozen as it had been yesterday. She wasn't sure whether that was a good thing or not, but she did her best to ignore it, especially as she watched Lucas, who looked completely unfazed by the fact that he was getting drenched as he slipped and slid down the steep slope to get closer to the huge black horse.

For the next hour, as the clouds continued to drizzle cold rain all over them, Kenzie watched in awe as Lucas spoke to the horse softly using the headlights from Ralph's truck as his main source of light due to the thick foliage surrounding the area where the horse had gotten stuck. Somehow he managed to keep her calm while Ralph called someone over at a place called Dead Heat Ranch. From what Kenzie gathered, Lucas's uncle and his five cousins — all girls — owned the place, and they had more than enough people to help.

After the new arrivals showed up a short time later, with Lucas still completely in charge, they managed to get the horse freed from the mud and back up on higher ground. Once that task was completed, Lucas ordered a couple of the ranch hands to put a temporary fix on the fence being that it was closing in on lunchtime, informing Ralph he'd be back out tomorrow to get it fixed properly once they could get the necessary materials.

Kenzie wasn't sure what she would've done had Lucas not been there. Not only had he been extremely cool under tremendous pressure, he'd never once acted as though he were put out by helping. She had heard Ralph thank one of the guys from Dead Heat Ranch, and the only response Ralph had received was, "That's what we do in small towns. We help each other."

It was then that Kenzie realized that Embers Ridge was exactly where she was supposed to be. Whether her grandfather had known it or not when he'd left the place to her, he had sealed her fate. Not only had he given her purpose and something to look forward to each and every day, he'd inadvertently brought her Lucas.

Although they'd only spent one day and one night together, she knew, without a doubt, that he'd been brought into her life for a reason. Now she just needed to make him understand how she felt, and she hoped like hell he didn't freak out for a third time in two days.

Once they were back at her house, Kenzie was completely soaked and shivering from the cold rain that had drenched her. Lucas seemed to know exactly what to do to fix that problem, too. After he turned up the heat, he led her back to her bathroom, where they took their second shower of the day. Together.

This time, they didn't linger past a few heated kisses, which worked wonders to heat her up from the inside out, finally thawing her out completely. Once they were finished, Kenzie made her way to the kitchen, once again wearing only her robe. While he finished up, she doctored her knee, which was doing significantly better than it had been the day before. She was surprised, considering all the things they'd done...

Her wandering thoughts made her blush.

"What are you thinkin' about?" Lucas asked when he walked into the kitchen.

"Nothin'," she told him, trying not to smile.

"Right. And I believe you based on how pink your cheeks are right now." Lucas came right over to her and pressed his lips to hers. "You're thinkin' about yesterday, aren't ya?"

"Are you a mind reader?" she asked teasingly.

"Maybe."

"Well, then what am I thinkin' right this minute?"

Lucas pulled back and looked at her. His expression went from lighthearted to serious in the blink of an eye, and Kenzie suddenly worried that he was going to figure out just where her thoughts had drifted.

"You're thinkin' the same thing I am," he finally said, his voice firm, lacking the humor it'd held just a few minutes ago.

"Yeah? And what are you thinking?" she questioned, suddenly hesitant to tell him what was on her mind.

Lucas cupped her face gently, his thumbs sliding over her cheeks, his eyes locked with hers. "I'm thinking that I want to see where this goes. Whatever this is… It just feels right."

"I agree," she said more confidently.

"I never believed…"

Lucas didn't finish his statement, and Kenzie wasn't sure where he had intended to go with it, but she picked up where his thoughts had gone. Figuring she might as well just get it out there. "Never believed in what? Love at first sight?"

"No, I never believed in love at first sight. Part of me doubted I'd ever believe in love again."

Her heart took on an entirely different beat in her chest as his thumbs continued to caress her cheeks. This strong, handsome, hesitant cowboy had just used the L word, and she wasn't sure what to do with that.

"But you're sayin' you do believe in love?" she asked, wanting to ensure she understood him correctly.

"That's what I'm sayin'."

"So, what if we don't think of it is as love at first sight?" Kenzie asked.

"What do we think of it as then?" Lucas asked, a small smile creeping up on his beautiful mouth.

Kenzie thought about that for a moment, and then it came to her. "Overnight love."

Lucas's smile grew bigger, making him even more handsome than before. Kenzie loved when he smiled.

"I like it," he told her.

"Well, then it's settled. Overnight love."

Lucas stared at her for a few seconds, his smile slipping. "It's forever with me, Kenzie. Do you think you can handle that?"

Kenzie pretended to consider that for a second. She didn't need to. Forever sounded pretty damn perfect for her. Especially if forever included him in it. "I can handle it, cowboy. Under one condition."

"What's that?" Lucas's face grew more serious.

Kenzie leaned up and pressed her lips to his gently. "I can handle it just as long as you can handle me."

"Darlin', I'm certainly up for the challenge."

Epilogue

Eighteen months later…

L ucas was sweating like a whore in church.

He was so damn nervous, and he had no fucking idea why. It wasn't like he hadn't known this day was coming. Hell, he'd had nine whole months to prepare for it, yet here he was, shaking like a leaf, willing his legs to hold him up while the doctor encouraged Kenzie to push.

"Lucas." The agony in Kenzie's voice tore at him, made him want to do whatever he could to take away her pain, but he knew there wasn't a damn thing he could do. He wasn't even able to remember any of those damn breathing techniques they'd learned in that class he'd gone to with her. The best he could offer his wife was his hand, and she was currently squeezing it until he was pretty sure the bones were rubbing together.

"One more time, Kenzie. You're doing great," the gray-haired doctor with the glasses told her. "Take a deep breath."

Kenzie didn't respond, but her grip tightened on his hand, and she groaned, doing just what the doctor told her while Lucas stood there like a dumbass.

"Good girl," the doctor said. "Almost there. Keep pushing."

There was a moment of silence, and Lucas watched the doctor. He could only see the top of his head because he was currently leaning over between Kenzie's spread thighs — which, had he not been a professional, would've gotten his teeth knocked in.

When the doctor looked up briefly, Lucas met his gaze. "Congratulations, you two," he said. "You've got a beautiful little girl."

And then … the entire world took on an entirely different hue.

Lucas could hardly breathe, could hardly hear past the roaring in his ears as he watched the doctor turn, handing off a slimy little bundle to a nurse who was standing directly beside him. She took the baby with care, doing whatever it was that nurses did when babies came out of their mothers. And then there was the most beautiful sound in the world, and the roaring dissipated, leaving Lucas listening to the sound of his daughter's cry.

"She's got your temper," Kenzie said, squeezing his hand, this time more gently than before.

Lucas smiled down at her, and when the nurse brought their daughter over and placed her in Kenzie's arms, he did the one thing he'd sworn he wouldn't do.

He cried.

"She's beautiful," Kenzie said softly. "Look at her, Lucas. She's got your nose."

Lucas looked at their daughter's tiny little nose, then up at Kenzie's face. He wasn't going to agree with her, because in his opinion, their daughter looked just like Kenzie. Just as beautiful, just as perfect.

His life was officially complete. Kenzie had walked into his life, setting his world to rights, making him a husband and now a father. She was truly a blessing he still wondered whether he deserved.

What had started out as an overnight love had morphed into something much greater.

Forever love.

Yes, that was what this was.

Forever.

□■□■□■□■

I hope you enjoyed Lucas and Kenzie's story. This novella is tied in with the Dead Heat Ranch series. If you'd like to keep up with the Dead Heat Ranch series, as well as all things Nicole Edwards, you can find out more on my website:

www.NicoleEdwardsAuthor.com.

Want to be notified of a new release? An author takeover? Where I'll be? Sign up for text messages on my website.

And last but certainly not least, if you want to see what's going on with me each week, sign up for my Hot Sheet on my website!

Enjoy ménage? Keep reading for an excerpt from

Nicole's Dead Heat Ranch series.

Boots *Optional*

Dead Heat Ranch

Nicole Edwards

Released July 22, 2014

Prologue

"What the hell?" Grant slurred as he stuck his head in the refrigerator, his plan for finding another beer not looking good. Either they'd already sucked them all down, or he was drunker than he thought. He doubted it was the latter, but the cool refrigerated air sweeping across his overheated skin told him he was feeling *something*.

Although "drunk" was a fantastic excuse, it wasn't likely the culprit.

"What's the problem?" Lane asked, poking his head damn near in the refrigerator beside Grant's, his powerful shoulder pressing up against his arm.

Grant jumped back, stumbled a couple of steps before he righted himself by grabbing the edge of the Formica countertop. He stared back at his friend, noticing the way Lane moved ever so slowly as he turned around to face Grant.

Yeah, that hadn't been at all subtle.

"Well, damn, Grant. I showered before I came over." Lane ducked his head near his armpit and sniffed. "Nope, I smell like an ocean breeze. Did you know that's what a fucking ocean breeze smells like?"

Grant fought the urge to smile. Lane did that to him. The man was always attempting to make him laugh but at the moment, he couldn't find much humor in the incredibly awkward situation he found himself in. "What're you talkin' about?" Grant asked, the room spinning just a little, but it had nothing to do with the alcohol swimming in his system.

Although he did need another beer. That or he needed for Lane to go home. Either option would work for him.

Shit.

Lane closed the refrigerator door just a little too hard, a couple of glass bottles clanking together as the door shut tight. Grant kept his eyes on the taller man, wishing like hell he hadn't opened the front door to let his friend in a couple of hours ago. Then again, everything had been fine as they sat in their respective recliners watching television up until about three minutes ago, but *no*, Grant had to go and need another beer.

Well, truthfully, everything *hadn't* been fine but at least Lane hadn't realized that. Grant was tense, but he seemed to always be that way around Lane. A reaction that had become increasingly more frustrating in recent months. Mostly due to the attraction he felt for the handsome wrangler who'd become one of his closest friends over the past couple of years.

"You got a problem with me, Kingsley?" Lane asked, his eyes dancing with amusement, his deep voice reverberating through Grant's entire body as the man moved closer. Incredibly close.

"Just need a beer," Grant said, his mouth suddenly dry.

"There's another six pack on the table." Lane motioned his head toward the kitchen table, his eyes never leaving Grant's face.

Grant made the mistake of looking over and sure enough, there was a six-pack of long neck bottles right there.

How the hell had he missed that?

When he looked back at Lane, the man was even closer. Close enough that yes, Grant was well aware that he had showered – and shaved – before he stopped by. He smelled good. Too good.

"You're actin' weird," Lane told him bluntly, tilting his head slightly as he studied Grant's face.

"Weird?" Grant asked stupidly, swallowing hard.

He wasn't acting weird. He was trying to drink himself into a stupor since that seemed to be the only way he could make it through any length of time around Lane without wanting to jump the man.

Snapping back to the present, Grant put his hands on Lane's chest, ready to shove his friend back because he was too damn close. Before he could do as much, Lane covered Grant's hands with his own, holding them to his chest and preventing Grant from putting any space between them.

Lane's heartbeat thudded rhythmically beneath Grant's palms.

Double shit.

"What are you doing?" Grant asked, though the words came out breathless and rough as he stared into Lane's dark, dark brown eyes.

"What do you think I'm doing?"

"Hell if I know," Grant lied. He knew exactly what Lane was doing and he'd be damned if he knew how to stop him, but that was only because he didn't *want* to stop him. Grant had dreamed about this moment, but he'd never thought it would actually happen.

Not with Lane. Not like this anyway.

Lane's chest was hard beneath his palms, his hands hot against the backs of his, and Grant found it rather difficult to breathe.

He hadn't had that much beer, damn it.

"Man, quit fucking with me," Grant bellowed, once again trying to push Lane away, pretending that he had no idea what was about to happen in three... two... one...

Oh, goddamn!

The instant Lane's mouth touched his, Grant lost all ability to shove him away; instead, he was reaching up, grasping Lane's hair in his fist and pulling him against him as the kiss exploded. Tongues, teeth, hands...

"Holy fuck," Lane mumbled long seconds later when he pulled back, looking directly into Grant's eyes before his mouth slammed into his once more.

Grant's entire body went hot, his cock hardening. And when Lane pushed up against him, successfully pinning Grant between the counter and his massive body, he was at a loss. The only thing he could do was kiss this man.

Kiss him and pray like hell that what they were doing wasn't the stupidest thing either of them had ever done.

To put it simply, Lane was shocked.

For one, he'd dreamed of this moment for months, never actually believing they would ever get to this point although they'd been doing some strange dance for about that long. Despite Grant's attempt to hide his desire, Lane had felt the heat of Grant's stare more than once.

And now, Grant had his hands in Lane's hair, pulling him closer while their tongues played hockey, dueling for control. Lane couldn't get enough of him. Grant tasted like beer and sex and – *holy fuck* – he wanted more.

With ease, Lane managed to spin them so that he was the one against the counter and Grant was in front of him. Holding him near while Grant continued to pull on his hair, Lane snaked his hand between their bodies and made quick work of releasing the button on Grant's jeans. Within seconds, he had the zipper down and Grant's jeans around his thighs. Oh, no, he wasn't going to let this moment go. Not if he had any say in the matter.

When Grant groaned, Lane wrapped his fingers around his thick cock, firmly gripping him. Just enough to let him know who was in control. Not that Lane had much control left. Not after tonight.

For nearly two hours, they'd sat in the living room laughing at the television while Grant had tried his best to ignore Lane at every turn. Lane knew how it worked, he knew what to expect from Grant, because the man wasn't going to outwardly pursue him, even if Lane begged. Yet here they were and his head was about to explode because he was touching Grant, kissing him.

Fuck. It was better than he anticipated.

"Holy shit," Grant moaned as he pulled back, his attention immediately turning to where Lane was stroking him slowly.

"Does it feel good?"

"Yeah," Grant breathed roughly. "Too good."

"And to think you've been avoiding this. Avoiding *me.*"

Lane didn't need Grant to admit it, he already knew the truth. But he'd promised himself that if they ever got to this point, he wouldn't let the moment pass him by.

Something caught his eye and Lane looked up to see…

Christ. There in the doorway – behind Grant – was Gracie Lambert. She was staring at them, clearly mesmerized to the point she didn't realize Lane knew she was there.

What he wouldn't give for her to take a chance and erase the twenty or so feet that stood between her and pleasure the likes of which none of them had ever known. But he knew Gracie. She wasn't going to act on any impulse, no matter how tempting the urge might be. She had been blowing them off since day one, and Lane figured that if she had her way, she'd continue to do so until hell froze over.

"Lane," Grant moaned, his head falling back as Lane continued to stroke him.

"I want to taste you," Lane admitted, his eyes still locked on Gracie, but she wasn't looking up at him. She was completely unaware that he was watching her, which made it that much hotter.

Grant didn't tell him no. He didn't try to pull away and fuck it all, Lane just wanted to take him in his mouth and blow his mind. Something to ease the pressure in hopes that Grant would see that there was something between them even if he were scared to admit it.

Lane forced Grant back a couple of steps, enough to give him room to go to his knees on the worn linoleum floor. Looking up at Grant, Lane continued to stroke him while the cowboy watched, his ocean blue eyes glazed with desire.

With ease, he darted his tongue out and lapped at the bead of pre-cum slicking the head of Grant's engorged cock. Another growl from Grant, and Lane sucked him fully into his mouth, their eyes still locked together.

Although he wasn't looking directly at her, Lane could still feel Gracie watching them. It wasn't that he needed any damned encouragement because shit, Grant was more than enough to make Lane hot, but he would admit that knowing the woman was standing there, probably heating up nicely from the free show going on before her, didn't hurt.

Grant's strong hand slid into Lane's hair, holding him firmly as Lane continued to suck him deep and then retreat. Over and over, he continued to lave Grant's dick while he fondled Grant's balls with one hand.

"God, Lane. Fuck. I've wanted you to do this for a long damn time."

Lane didn't comment. He just sucked harder, deeper, faster.

"Fuck yes," Grant groaned, his hand clutching Lane's hair painfully tight, sending shards of electricity through his scalp. "God, don't stop. Don't ever fucking stop."

Grant didn't have to worry there. Lane had wanted to get his hands on Grant for a long damn time. He also wanted to get his hands on the sweet cowgirl still watching them from the shadows of the front porch. He'd openly admitted to the latter, but never had he out and out admitted the intensity of his desire for Grant.

Not until tonight.

"God damn," Grant howled. "You're gonna make me come. Fuck. You're gonna…"

That's exactly what Lane was going for. At least for tonight. Tonight was about Grant.

And the sexy cowgirl who might not yet realize just what she'd gotten herself into.

Enjoy ménage? Keep reading for an excerpt from
Nicole's standalone novel:

A Million Tiny Pieces

Nicole Edwards

Released January 20, 2015

Prologue

AFTER THE SUDDEN death of his father three months ago, venture capitalist Phoenix Pierce has become the youngest team owner in NHL history. We are here to announce that, with the NHL board of governors' official approval, Phoenix's minority share in the Austin Arrows combined with his father's majority share now puts twenty-nine-year-old Pheonix at the helm of the Arrows organization.

When recently asked whether there would be changes to the team in the upcoming season, Phoenix advised that there had already been plans in the works prior to Sidney Pierce's death. Sid died suddenly from a heart attack back in May.

From what we've learned from Tarik Marx, the public relations spokesperson for the Arrows, Phoenix intends to implement those changes and move forward. He has assured us that the team is healthy and strong and looking forward to a solid year ahead.

Phoenix refused to comment further on the pending lawsuit from real estate mogul Damien Landry. According to our sources, prior to Sid's death, there was a rumor that the team was to be sold to Landry for a reported $280 million. Forbes.com recently valued the Arrows at $205 million, although the team has reported an estimated $10 million loss each year due to its continued decline in rankings.

We were told by a source close to Landry that Sid had backed out of the deal two months prior to his death; however, no documentation has been provided to support Landry's claim. Yet Landry refuses to go away quietly.

As Tarik made his way into the room, Phoenix hit the button on the remote to turn off the television, causing the darkened room to be cloaked in silence.

Dropping onto the arm of the sofa, Tarik forced a smile as he watched his boss stare at the blank TV screen. It was far too early in the morning to be drinking, but since neither of them had gone to sleep yet, it was fitting.

Twisting so that he could face Phoenix, Tarik held up his beer bottle. "You're in full control now. It might be bittersweet, but it's still a win."

"Bittersweet," Phoenix echoed, not bothering to look up from where he was slumped on the sofa as he blindly held up his beer bottle, clanking it with Tarik's. "Bitter-*fucking*-sweet."

»»»»»» ♥ «««««

MIA CANTRELL PROPPED her shoulder against the wall, staring out one of the floor-to-ceiling windows of the high-rise condominium she had recently purchased and moved into as she willed her fluttering heart to settle. Kings of Leon softly crooned through the speakers in her living room but did little to ease the tension that had been building for the last few days.

With her second cup of coffee warming her hands, she watched the sun peek over the Austin skyline laid out before her, trying to get a grip on herself. It would've been decidedly easier if she weren't pondering how her life had gone so wrong.

Wrong? No, wait. She tossed the word around in her mouth for a moment but didn't like the feel. Maybe *wrong* wasn't necessarily the appropriate word.

Touching her lips with the tips of her fingers, Mia realized she was smiling. Now that she thought about it, she was inclined to say that she was actually quite content for the first time in a very long time, even excited about her new lease on life. So maybe it was more accurate to use the word *different* in this case.

Yes … things were now so very *different.*

Moving her hand to her chest, she noticed her heart had finally stopped pounding, although she could still feel the anxious flutter in her tummy.

As soon as she had crawled into bed last night, she had realized how eager she was for this day to start. Naturally, that excitement had carried over into her dreams. Two hours ago, just as Mia had done in grade school when her mother would wake her on the first day of a new school year, she had practically leaped out of bed. But not from her mother's sweet words or her mother's gentle hand nudging her awake. Nope, Mia's alarm clock had belted out a noise — one that should be illegal in at least half the country — that got her moving today. It had had the same effect a fire alarm would have. She had thrown off the covers, shot upright out of her bed before she'd even realized she was awake.

As she'd learned that morning, it was vastly different getting ready these days than it had been for the last few years. When it wasn't necessary to get perfectly coifed, lacquered, and spit-shined, things were considerably easier. After drying her hair, Mia had realized that she didn't need to curl her long blonde locks. And when she went to put on her makeup, she recognized it was not necessary to accentuate her bright blue eyes with tons of eyeliner and mascara, either. She wasn't that girl anymore.

So, instead of spending an extra hour polishing herself to perfection, Mia had pulled her hair back into a ponytail, secured it in place with a brightly colored rubber band, applied a clear gloss to her lips, and pulled on her favorite outfit these days — jeans and an oversized, comfy T-shirt.

What was left was a much younger woman staring back at her, and she happened to like the new image. This new version of herself … well, she seemed less confined, less restricted.

Significantly more confident.

As far as Mia was concerned, this was exactly where she was meant to be. And in a few minutes, she would be taking the next steps in jump-starting the rest of her life.

Her first day of college.

Chapter One

January

"GOOD MORNING, MR. Pierce," Phoenix's doorman, George, greeted, holding the glass door open to allow him to enter when he strolled up to the building.

Strolled. Right. Because *that* was what he was doing.

Waving him off briefly, Phoenix stopped inside the lobby to catch his breath. Folding himself over, he pressed his hands to his knees and sucked in oxygen as though the world were in short supply. His lungs happened to feel as though it really was.

These days, his hour-long morning runs were getting the best of him. During the particularly brutal form of hell that he'd put himself through today, Phoenix had finally convinced himself that this was another kind of self-punishment that he was allowing to get out of hand.

Not that he planned to do anything about that — he had merely accepted it.

"Good morning, George," Phoenix replied when he could form words and not sound like a vacuum hose stuck to a pillow.

George smiled down at him. "I didn't realize you were back in town, Mr. Pierce. Will you be here for a while?"

"Nope," he answered, the only word he could shove past his constricted lungs. Forcing his tired muscles to return him to his full height, he slapped the air fleetingly, an exhausted form of a wave, and headed toward the elevators that would take him to the penthouse.

"Good morning, Mr. Pierce," Roy, the elderly man who prided himself on manning the front desk, said cheerfully as he punched the up arrow on the wall to call the elevator. "The other elevator's on the fritz again. We've called a repairman, so hopefully it'll be back to normal in a bit."

Phoenix nodded in Roy's direction, still trying to preserve what oxygen he did have. He didn't really care about the status of the elevators, but he wasn't going to tell Roy that.

Instead, he walked in a circle on the gray travertine floor, hands on his hips, chest still rising and falling rapidly, trying to keep his muscles from locking up as he watched the numbers above the elevator doors, waiting for the next car to arrive. It had momentarily paused at seventeen and was down to two before he stopped pacing and stood stone still, hoping like hell his quads weren't going to do some sort of new trick and refuse to stretch enough to walk.

Phoenix dropped his gaze to the floor, allowing his hood to cover most of his face, not wanting to make eye contact with whomever was coming off the elevator. Today was not the day for a complete stranger to want to engage him in a conversation about hockey, something he found himself doing more and more often these days.

When the doors opened, the first thing he saw was a pair of running shoes. They were too small to belong to a man, so he allowed his gaze to travel north slowly.

Very slowly.

A pair of trim, jean-clad legs came into view. And as he continued his path upward, moving on to admire the small, curvy hips attached to the impressive legs, he found himself skipping over the oversized sweatshirt until he met a pair of crystal-blue eyes staring back at him. From this distance, those eyes seemed to glow — a brilliant turquoise, so clear, so pure that the color was probably only rivaled by that of the waters of the Caribbean.

"Excuse me," the succulent mouth attached to the beautiful face that held the bright blue eyes said.

Those words had Phoenix's gaze sliding back down to her lips. Perfect pink lips that he noticed were *not* forming a smile.

Well, hell.

Phoenix nodded his head — a nonverbal form of an apology — knowing there was no sense trying to force the words out through his abused lungs. Although now they were oxygen deficient because this woman had taken his breath away, not because he'd run nine miles.

Phoenix couldn't look away as she moved around him, giving him a wide berth, those striking blue eyes tracking his every move as though he might jump on her at the first possible chance.

Oh, jumping on her was definitely on his mind, but not in the way she was probably imagining. Phoenix was suddenly thinking about naked acrobatics, actually. Some slick, sweaty sex that resulted in those blue eyes piercing his as he made her come a hundred different ways, in a thousand different positions.

He realized he was still staring at her, watching the gentle sway of her sweet, heart-shaped ass encased in lucky fucking denim. He wanted to be her fucking jeans at that moment.

The elevator dinged, and Phoenix turned back to see the doors were beginning to close. He shoved his arm in to stop them, waving Roy off, not wanting to wait another five minutes for the damn thing to return. As he backed into the car, he watched the sexy blonde smile at George as they engaged in a short conversation.

He wanted to be George.

Okay, no. He did *not* fucking want to be George.

But Phoenix did have every intention of talking to George a little later. After all, he wanted to know who those blue eyes belonged to. Apparently the doorman knew her well enough to earn a sweet smile before the woman moved closer to the door.

When she stepped out onto the street and out of his line of sight, Phoenix punched in a code that would take him to the penthouse. As the elevator doors closed, effectively blocking any opportunity of seeing the woman who was responsible for kicking his heart rate back up into dangerous territory, he gave in to his exhaustion and allowed the wall to hold him up.

Jesus Christ, he was acting like a fucking teenage boy. He really needed to get a grip.

The elevator ride to the top floor was as painful as waiting for the damn thing on the first floor, and by the time the doors slid open, Phoenix was desperate to get out of the steel box. He stepped into the lavish entry that smelled oddly of cinnamon for reasons unbeknownst to him, and after crossing the vast space that separated his door from the elevator, he punched in another code to gain entry to his condo.

Nudging the door open a fraction of an inch, he glanced back over his shoulder, trying to locate the source of the smell. It had to be his mother's doing — that was the only logical explanation — but for the life of him, Phoenix had no idea what the hell it could be. The only thing he noticed — with the exception of all the Christmas decorations having finally been taken down — was a bowl of pinecones resting on the antique table that sat between the two sets of elevator doors.

Did pinecones smell like cinnamon? Surely not.

Realizing he truly didn't give a shit, Phoenix grabbed the knob and pushed open the front door to his condo.

When he stepped inside, he was breathing regularly and his heart was no longer trying to crack through a rib. He grabbed the stack of mail that was sitting on the table inside the door, the same place his bodyguard/public relations spokesman/assistant, Tarik Marx, put it every day.

The guy had too many fucking job titles, that was all there was to it.

As usual, Phoenix took a moment to flip through the envelopes, not finding any of them especially appealing. Tossing them back on the table, he glanced in the mirror hanging on the wall in front of him.

Damn. No wonder the blue-eyed woman had given him a wide berth as she'd come off the elevator. The black hoodie he wore covered most of his head, and the little bit of his face that was visible looked downright lethal. His black hair fell across his forehead, his green eyes glittered, probably from the pain and suffering of having pushed himself to his limits that morning. Hell, even his nose looked a little more crooked than normal. Scrubbing his hands over his jaw, he realized he needed to shave.

Hopefully, he'd had the decency to smile when she had been standing there, allowing him to eye fuck her first thing in the morning. Knowing him, he hadn't. He didn't smile much these days, mainly because it took too much fucking effort.

"Phoenix, is that you?"

"If it's not, then I may have to question who you let in here, Mother," Phoenix replied, snatching the mail up once more and flipping through it again. Anything to look busy.

His mother made it her job to visit him every morning. She had her own condo in the same building, yet she arrived at some point after Phoenix left for his daily run, and she stuck around for a short time after he got back, longer if he didn't appear to have anything to do. Not that he didn't love his mother, but despite what she thought, he really was busy.

Too busy.

"Don't you get smart with me, young man."

Smiling to himself, Phoenix didn't respond.

His mother must've known he had no retort, because she added, "Tarik should be here any minute."

"Yes, he should. And your point?" he asked, keeping his eyes on the envelopes and making his way through the vast, open area that served as a living room, dining room, and den.

His condo consisted of the entire thirty-sixth floor. Roughly five thousand square feet overlooking downtown Austin in a building he personally owned that housed three hundred and forty additional condominiums. It should've been enough space to keep him from having to run into someone every time he walked through the door, especially since he lived alone, but that never seemed to be the case.

With one eye still on his mail, Phoenix stepped into the commercial-grade kitchen, feeling his mother's eyes track him as he stopped in front of the refrigerator.

Sometimes Phoenix wished Tarik didn't feel the need to go down to the gym every morning while Phoenix went for his morning run. If the guy would come to work first thing, Phoenix would be spared this awkward daily confrontation with his mother. Most of the time, Phoenix was back before Tarik arrived, which meant he was left dealing with his mother alone.

Tossing the less-than-interesting envelopes onto the black granite counter for Tarik to deal with later, Phoenix flipped the hood off his head, opened the refrigerator, and grabbed two single bottles of orange juice. He had learned long ago that drinking out of the carton — although he was the only one drinking from it — was a surefire way to get his mother to ride his ass first thing in the morning.

Tarik's solution: individual bottles.

Phoenix couldn't argue with the man's logic. Wasn't the first time he'd thought Tarik was a genius, either.

As he tipped the first bottle to his lips, Phoenix glanced at his mother. As always, Ellen Pierce was dressed in one of her beloved black silk pantsuits, her short ebony hair, severely cut and board straight, resting on her shoulders. While Phoenix watched her, those observant green eyes, so similar to his own, raked over his face.

"Are you here to stay for a while?" Ellen asked.

Phoenix shook his head. "On the road this week."

His mother didn't respond immediately, simply watched him carefully. Studying him silently.

She was always trying to figure him out. He'd informed her on more than one occasion that it wasn't worth the time or effort. Half the time, he couldn't predict what he would do or say next; no sense in someone else trying to do the same.

In his defense, Phoenix was only unpredictable as long as it didn't have to do with business. When it came to his companies, he was as straightforward as he was shrewd and single-minded. At twenty-nine, he'd built an empire that couldn't be rivaled by many, and he didn't make any apologies for it, either. It hadn't come easy, but it had helped that his father — God rest his soul — had taught him everything he knew before he'd died nine months ago. A fresh wave of grief passed through him as he thought about his father. God, he missed him more with each day that passed.

But he'd had little time to grieve for the man who'd been his mentor and role model. After Sidney Pierce had suffered a heart attack that'd taken his life and stolen the person Phoenix had been closest to in the world, he'd been hard-pressed to move forward, to keep things going in the right direction, to prove to himself — as much as to his father — that he was worthy.

Now that Phoenix was the owner of the Austin Arrows, one of the youngest teams in the NHL, as well as Pierce Industries, a multi-million-dollar venture capitalist firm, he didn't have nearly as much time for erratic, impulsive behavior as he'd once had.

As he figured it, either the job was getting to him or he was getting old.

He refused to believe the latter.

Twisting the lid off the second bottle of juice, Phoenix said, "We'll have dinner next weekend. Will that work?"

The smile that formed on his mother's ageless features brightened her entire face. "I'd like that."

Draining the second bottle of juice, Phoenix tossed both bottles and the lids into the recycle bin, knowing Tarik would have his ass if he didn't. Sometimes he threw them in the trash solely to listen to him bitch and moan.

It was the little things that got Phoenix going in the morning.

"I've got to shower," he informed his mother. "Then I've got a meeting at the office."

Ellen nodded. She of all people knew he wasn't much of a morning person, and standing around waiting for him to spark a conversation before he'd had his first cup of coffee was like waiting for him to find any interest in a woman for more than one night.

It just didn't happen.

Leaving his mother in the living room, Phoenix escaped to his bedroom, locking the door behind him.

»»»»»» ♥ «««««

WITH HER SUNGLASSES shielding her face, Mia stepped out onto the sidewalk, the blustery January wind slapping her in the face, instantly freezing her nose. As she fought the overwhelming urge to turn around and sneak a peek at the guy she'd passed on her way out of the elevator, she gave a cursory glance around to see if any reporters were lurking nearby. She was happy to see that today must've been a big news day elsewhere, meaning she was alone.

Don't look back. Don't look back. Don't…

Luckily the windows on the building were reflective, and even if she attempted to look inside, it would be futile, so she shrugged off the notion. She reminded herself that she didn't have time for men, especially intimidating ones whose faces she couldn't even see thanks to the hood that had been covering his head.

As she passed the coffee shop next door, she wished she had a few minutes to go in and grab a coffee to go, but she knew she was going to be late if she didn't hurry. With winter break now over, she had learned last week that her professors had a renewed sense of vigor when it came to keeping things on track. She wondered how long that would last. Regardless, she didn't want to be late for class.

As she pulled her hood over her ears and ducked her head, Mia smiled to herself. Oh, how things had changed from a year ago. If all those people could see her now, battling the elements as she walked to school rather than having someone chauffeur her around... She knew that her story had probably been heard before: lonely young wife of a rich and powerful man finds herself kicked off the pedestal she'd once been put on, forced to move back into a regular routine, without the glitz and glamor that had been an integral part of her everyday life ... blah, blah, blah.

But that's where her story began to differ.

At least she'd like to think that was the case.

First of all, no longer wed to the insufferable asshole, Mia had shunned her married name and taken back her maiden name. So that made her the *ex*-wife of a rich and powerful man — a crucial piece to the new puzzle that was her life.

Secondly, the glitz still seemed to be following her around, but only if the bright flash of cameras constantly in her face whenever she walked out of her building and on the street could be considered being in the limelight. For whatever reason, they wouldn't leave her alone. *They* being the paparazzi. It seemed there were still some people out to get the juicy dirt on one of the most newsworthy businessmen in the great state of Texas, Damien Landry. Mia's ex-husband.

And they were apparently accomplishing that goal by following her around. Well, except for today, which was a nice change of pace.

How much did you get in the divorce, Mia?

Are you upset that Damien has moved on?

Did you actually catch him in bed with another woman?

Can you tell us about the lawsuit, Mia?

What will you do now, Ms. Cantrell?

She'd heard all the questions a million times over, but every time she answered with the same: "I'm not married to him anymore. Not sure what he's doing."

They didn't listen. But she wasn't surprised.

Whatever floozy was hanging on Damien's arm at this point should have to deal with all of their constant harassment, not her. She'd relinquished that burden when Damien had come home from a business trip reeking of perfume. *Cheap* perfume, at that. Since Mia knew he hadn't taken to wearing it, she had assumed that it belonged to another woman. And truthfully, she knew Damien was not that stupid, which meant he'd wanted her to catch him. From the beginning, Mia had warned him that cheating was a deal breaker for her. He had called her bluff.

He had quickly learned that she wasn't bluffing.

And here she was — officially single as of two months ago, when her divorce was final — crossing one of the busy downtown Austin streets on her way to the University of Texas campus, wondering how she'd ended up, now twenty-four years old, back where she'd started.

Granted, Mia wasn't the same naïve young girl she'd been when she'd first met Damien. No, that twenty-year-old virgin had long since disappeared, in her place a woman who was much smarter, much less gullible.

At least she'd like to think so.

Being married to Damien might've robbed her of her innocence, made her into a woman she hadn't recognized for the last few years, but Mia couldn't blame him for everything. She'd been a willing participant. Right up to the moment she'd told him that she wanted a divorce — nine months ago.

Looking back on it now, Mia realized it hadn't been all that difficult to fall for an attractive, wealthy man like Damien. He was older, some would say far too old for a twenty-year-old girl who, at the time, had still been living at home with her mother while she plotted out the rest of her life. Unfortunately, she hadn't figured out until later — much, much later — how true that really was.

At twenty, Mia hadn't been even remotely old enough to handle being married to a man like Damien. Hell, even now she questioned whether she was mentally strong enough to deal with the emotional upheaval he was known for.

That never stopped her from trying to make it work. The way she saw it, marriage was supposed to be forever. Apparently, she and Damien hadn't been reading from the same book when it came to the sanctity of their wedding vows.

She had met Damien on a Friday night at a restaurant in downtown Austin where Mia had been having a celebratory dinner with some of her closest friends. They'd all been gearing up to start college in the fall after taking a year off to enjoy themselves, something Mia's mother had advised her against. But in her opinion, she'd needed a break. And when she'd met Damien, she'd been ready to grow up, ready to move on to the next phase of her life, school be damned.

At the time she'd started dating Damien, he'd been a young thirty-three, as he'd liked to tell it, thirteen years her senior. He was single, rich, and known for his playboy status. Not to mention, he'd avoided marriage on multiple occasions. Or so he'd proudly informed her.

According to him, he'd been waiting for the right woman. Her.

Rolling her eyes, Mia realized how silly that sounded thinking back on it now. Yes, she'd definitely been naïve and gullible at the time, hanging on every sweet word he'd told her until he'd charmed her right out of her panties two weeks after they'd met.

Although Mia hadn't intended to skip a large portion of young adulthood and move right into marriage, she'd found that Damien was a very persuasive man. He was handsome and charming, and she'd been putty in his hands from the very beginning. The media had made them out to be the perfect couple, and Mia had been too naïve to know what she was getting herself into. She'd been a beautiful blonde trophy — their words, not hers — on the arm of a man who was continuing to prove himself as a power player in the real estate market. At the time, Mia had felt like she was right up there on top of the world with him.

Her mother had warned her, but at the time, Mia had thought she was too overprotective, something Clarice Cantrell had been for most of Mia's life. So, Mia had done what any inexperienced twenty-year-old girl would do when faced with that sort of challenge: she'd ignored her mother's reasoning, insisting that she knew what she was doing.

Yeah, well, it wasn't the first time Mia would have to admit that she'd been wrong.

Unfortunately, her mother had been forced to sit back and watch her. And just as she'd predicted — something she'd later told Mia — Clarice had watched Mia climb, only to see her fall back down to earth, her broken heart in her hands.

However … what Mia's mother didn't understand was that her heart didn't have anything to do with it. Not in the end. Not after having endured all of the hardships living with Damien had brought her. No, what no one else seemed to realize was that Mia's heart had been shattered into a million tiny pieces long before that night.

Her marriage to the enigmatic man had proven to be the opposite of the fairy tale she'd thought it would be. She'd fallen in love with a blond-haired, blue-eyed charmer in the beginning, there was no doubt about that. But by the third year, Mia had watched her life crumble around her, and she'd known it wouldn't be long before she would have no choice but to get out. She'd decided at that time to reclaim her heart, even before she reclaimed her life.

Still, there were tiny fragments of her heart that she feared would never be put back in their original place, no matter how much she despised Damien, no matter how grateful she was to be able to move on.

Thankfully, Mia had planned for the worst, and she'd run fast and hard toward the infinitesimal light at the end of the tunnel in the end.

There had been a prenuptial agreement, but only because Mia had suggested it.

Seriously, the man was worth millions; it should've been Damien who had insisted on the legality. Nope, that'd been her.

She knew that was about the only reasonable thing she'd requested going into the relationship, and that was *after* her mother had broken down and cried. Mia was giving up her college years to be with a man who insisted that he be the one to take care of her, so, according to her mother, she should at least have something in writing to ensure she didn't have to start completely over.

She and Damien had worked out an agreement with the help of his ruthless lawyers so that she would get one million dollars for every birthday she spent married to the man — a mere crumb off the loaf of the Landry fortune — provided the marriage ended amicably. She'd spent three birthdays with him, would've been four had he not come home smelling like cheap perfume two weeks before her twenty-fourth birthday. Even knowing what she was giving up, Mia had left him the very next day with a suitcase packed full of her most beloved items and nothing else.

There had also been a clause that stated she would get an additional ten million if Damien cheated on her. At the time, Mia hadn't considered the fact that she would have to be able to *prove* the latter. Of course, the floozy on his arm these days wasn't admitting to anything, so she and Damien had agreed to disagree. It'd been easier on Mia just to let it all go and walk away. After all, cheating really was a deal breaker as far as she was concerned, and his admission had been enough for her. So, because she'd wanted out, she'd ended the marriage stating irreconcilable differences, and she'd walked away with three million dollars.

From the second the ink was dry on the divorce papers and the funds made it to her bank account, she'd become incredibly frugal with her money, despite her one and only splurge — the condo she now called home. Mia had plans, and that money would help her accomplish her goals and keep her from having to live with her mother until she could get to the point where she was financially stable. It would eventually be gone, and she didn't have any preconceived notions that she would ever make the kind of money that Damien did, nor would she run in the same circles that she had previously, but she was okay with that. She simply wanted to be happy, and for the first time in as long as she could remember, she was.

Which was how Mia had gotten to where she was now, walking up the steps on the UT campus, on her way to her first class of the day. She was probably a little too anxious, especially since she'd been doing this exact same thing for going on five months now, but she couldn't help herself. It'd been a long time since she'd had something like this to look forward to. But that was where she found herself. Looking forward to another day of school.

College.

How it had happened, she didn't know, but she'd been accepted at the University of Texas, and back in August, Mia had taken the necessary steps to move on with the rest of her life. Pursuing her degree in psychology, she was taking control of her destiny, no longer being led around by the nose, flaunted as a trophy, looked at as though she didn't have a brain cell in her head.

Each day seemed like her first day all over again, and she prayed the excitement didn't dwindle.

When Mia had first started school, she hadn't known what to expect because she'd been out of the loop for so long. Spending day and night with high society had left her with a detachment to the norm, which she'd longed to get back. She was glad to say that she had.

Opening the door to the building, Mia smiled to herself. Yep, this was a new day, another chance to keep moving forward, to live in the moment. What the future held, she didn't know. For now, she was going to embrace life. Embrace the woman she was becoming.

About Nicole

New York Times and *USA Today* bestselling author Nicole Edwards lives in Austin, Texas with her husband, their three kids, and four rambunctious dogs. When she's not writing about sexy alpha males, Nicole can often be found with her Kindle in hand or making an attempt to keep the dogs happy. You can find her hanging out on Facebook and interacting with her readers - even when she's supposed to be writing.

Website: **www.NicoleEdwardsAuthor.com**

Facebook: www.facebook.com/Author.Nicole.Edwards

Twitter: www.twitter.com/NicoleEAuthor

Nicole also writes contemporary/new adult romance as Timberlyn Scott.

By Nicole Edwards

The Alluring Indulgence Series
Kaleb
Zane
Travis
Holidays with the Walker Brothers
Ethan
Braydon
Sawyer
Brendon

The Austin Arrows Series
Rush
Kaufman

The Bad Boys of Sports Series
Bad Reputation
Bad Business

The Caine Cousins Series
Hard to Hold
Hard to Handle

The Club Destiny Series
Conviction
Temptation
Addicted
Seduction
Infatuation
Captivated
Devotion
Perception
Entrusted
Adored
Distraction

The Coyote Ridge Series
Curtis
Jared

The Dead Heat Ranch Series
Boots Optional
Betting on Grace
Overnight Love

By Nicole Edwards (cont.)

The Devil's Bend Series

Chasing Dreams
Vanishing Dreams

The Devil's Playground Series

Without Regret
Without Restraint

The Office Intrigue Series

Office Intrigue
Intrigued Out of the Office
Their Rebellious Submissive

The Pier 70 Series

Reckless
Fearless
Speechless
Harmless

The Sniper 1 Security Series

Wait for Morning
Never Say Never
Tomorrow's Too Late

The Southern Boy Mafia Series

Beautifully Brutal
Beautifully Loyal

Standalone Novels

A Million Tiny Pieces
Inked on Paper

Writing as Timberlyn Scott

Unhinged
Unraveling
Chaos

Naughty Holiday Editions

2015
2016

www.ingramcontent.com/pod-product-compliance
Lightning Source LLC
Chambersburg PA
CBHW060936120626
46557CB00003B/1024